The Adventures of Finnian The Leprechaun

Bradley Tolhurst

The Adventures of Finnian The Leprechaun

Table of Contents

1.

Bryan Melrose loved being in the scouts, and he loved camping, especially on nights like this one next to a roaring fire with the woodland just twenty metres away. It was a cool night in late March. Him and a couple of friends were cooking sausages on the fire, suspended from small twigs. His friend Peter Wright cursed as he dropped a small sausage into the fire, where the flames quickly consumed it.

"I was looking forward to that, " he spat in annoyance.

Michael Knowles, Bryan's best friend was looking delighted as a perfectly cooked sausage turned on his stick.

"You should cook them like this," he said.

Bryan finished his sausage, only slightly cold in the middle and looked towards the nearby woodland. "Who wants to go for a walk in the woods?" he asked his two friends.

"Yeah, why not? It's not too late yet," Michael replied, looking at his watch. "Only 7:30. Are the scoutmasters drinking again?" he added.

"Yeah, probably. I saw them drinking lager earlier," Peter responded. "I think they've had a skinful."

"So, they won't bother us then," Bryan replied, getting to his feet.

"What are you expecting to see in the woods?" Peter asked.

"Lions, obviously. Don't be an idiot. It will just be fun to look around," Bryan answered.

Eventually, the three boys, all aged eleven, finished their sausages and walked towards the woods. The scoutmaster's tent was off to the left, and the three men in charge were drinking and rambling to themselves. They didn't look up at the boys.

"We might see a fox," Peter said.

"Must be something more interesting than that," Michael snapped back.

"Like what?"

"I dunno. Maybe one of those big cats that live in the countryside."

"I'd bet you a million pounds you won't see one of them," Peter scoffed. "There's no evidence they exist."

"Well, let's just find out," Bryan said, pulling out his torch and pointing it ahead of them.

The three boys walked into the woods, their feet crackling on leaves and broken twigs. Bryan shone his torch around as the darkness was starting to get thicker.

"Don't go too far in," Peter said. "If we get lost, everyone will be angry with us."

"Just stick together, and we can help each other get out," Michael said abruptly.

For several minutes, the boys surveyed the woods. The trees were not particularly thick as spring hadn't really taken effect just yet. A few birds fluttered in front of them, and at one point, they saw a hedgehog which darted quickly away. Bryan considered climbing a tree to get an idea of how big the woods were when something suddenly dropped out of a tree in front of them. The three boys gasped and staggered back, with Bryan shining his torch on what looked like a large green melon. Soon, the boys realised that the green that they saw were the clothes belonging to a ridiculously small man who was rolling on the ground.

"What is it?" Peter yelled in alarm.

"You mean, who is it?" Bryan yelled back. "Looks like a small man."

"A small man?" a voice cut in from the writhing figure on the ground in a musical Irish lilt. The character sat up and perused the three intruders. The boys stared at him, open-mouthed in disbelief through the torchlight. "Have you not seen one of the little people before?"

The boys stood in silence as the little man sat up against a thin tree in front of them. He was all dressed in green with a ginger-coloured beard and a bald head. His green top hat lay on the ground nearby.

"That's not possible," Michael gasped. "He looks like a leprechaun."

"Oh, what?" Peter retorted. "Those things don't exist."

"Don't exist?" the man replied. "I, Finnian Coghlan, five thousand years old and born in Glendalough, Ireland, don't exist? I've never been so insulted."

Bryan laughed. "No way. Hey can you get us some gold?"

"Gold?" Finnian replied. "You think I'll just give you my gold when you say I don't exist?"

"If you're from Ireland, what are you doing in Kent?" Michael asked with a grin.

"I travel all over," said the little man, getting up and placing his hat on his head. "For someone who doesn't exist, I've seen a lot of the world."

The three boys laughed.

"This is amazing," commented Bryan. "What sort of things can you do?"

"What can't I do more, " Finnian replied. "I can do miracles. I could change the world if I wanted to."

"Why don't you then?" asked Peter. "Does this mean there's a God?"

"There's a God if you believe in him, and no God if you don't," he enigmatically replied.

The boys gave each other a puzzled look. "Are you really five thousand years old?" Bryan asked.

"As sure as you're eleven."

"I am eleven."

The boys looked at each other in surprise.

"How did you know that?"

"Because I'm very clever. Now, are you going to bombard me with questions all evening or explain what you want from me?"

Michael looked at his friends excitedly. "I heard that leprechauns can grant wishes. Three of them."

"Three if I feel like it. None if I don't," Finnian answered dryly.

"We can change the world, guys," Bryan exclaimed. "He can do anything for us."

Finnian didn't answer and began to climb the tree he'd recently fallen out of. He ascended high into the branches. He looked at the three boys from his position with a look of disinterest on his face.

"Please grant us three wishes. "Peter shouted up at him. "Or give us your pot of gold."

"You want my gold? Here it is." Finnian waved his right hand in the air, and a shower of dust cascaded onto the boys. It was gold-coloured and made the boys choke and splutter.

"What is this?" Bryan gasped. "This is gold coloured but not gold."

"And it's all the gold you'll be getting." Finnian yelled. "Rude, selfish boys get no more from me."

At that moment, Bryan pulled out his smartphone and pointed it up at the little man. "I can get him on film and sell it to the papers," he told his two friends.

With lightning speed, the leprechaun suddenly dashed down the tree, grabbed Bryan's phone from him and then scampered back to the height of it. "Oh no, you won't, you mischievous scamp," he called in defiance.

"Give me back my phone!" Bryan yelled.

"Why don't we chop down the tree, Bryan?" Peter asked.

"What with you moron?" Michael answered.

"If we catch him, he has to grant us three wishes," Peter answered quickly.

Finnian was now climbing even higher in the tree. There was no way the boys could

reach him.

"Why don't we tell our scoutmasters to help catch him?" Michael asked.

"Oh yeah. Can you help us catch a leprechaun up a tree? They'll send for the men in white coats." Bryan scoffed.

"He'll be gone when we get back anyway," Peter chipped in. "We have to do something now."

"You can't catch me," Finnian yelled happily, "You'll never get my wishes or my gold, but here's your phone."

At that point, Bryan's phone plummeted to the ground, striking a branch on the way down and shattering on the woodland floor.

"Why you. . ." Bryan raged. And tried to start climbing the tree himself, but he couldn't get any footholds and fell to the ground red-faced and panting.

"It's no good mate. We'll never catch him," Michael sighed.

Then, a moment later, they heard footsteps behind them, and another torch shone through the dark. It was their scoutmaster, Kevin Williams, moving quickly over.

"What the hell are you boys doing out here in the woods? It's not safe. Get back to camp right now," he barked. He was a large bald man and currently looked fierce and angry. The boys looked at him and then looked at each other.

"We're sorry, but. . . we. ." Bryan tailed off and then looked up into the tree. He could see the little man faintly but was sure Kevin wouldn't believe him if he pointed him out.

"Something up the tree?" Kevin asked, shining his torch into the branches above and looking up. The three boys went quiet. "I don't see anything up there."

"We thought you were all drinking," Peter said, and Michael kicked his shin.

"Oh, were you now?" Kevin yelled back. "You cheeky blighters, I'll tell your parents about this."

"You'll never get my gold, you cheeky scamps." the voice called from the tree and the boys were shaken into excited grins.

"Who was that?" Kevin asked, looking up at the tree. "Who's up there?" he shouted into the canopy. He fell silent, waiting for a reply.

The boys were whispering in excitement. "I can see someone," he said to the boys.

"It's a lep.." Michael began and then fell silent. He didn't know how to finish the sentence.

"A what?" Kevin yelled. "What are you boys doing with strange people in the woods?"

A second later, there was ruffling in the branches, and the four of them could see a shape hurtling towards them from above. Kevin leapt back as the tiny man jumped off the tree and stood in front of them. "Did I hear you say, strange people?" Finnian asked the scoutmaster. His face stern.

"Oh my God," Kevin babbled. "Who the hell are you?" and the three boys laughed to themselves.

"I'm a leprechaun, my good man, or maybe not so good man. So, which are you, a good man or not?"

Kevin didn't reply, and he turned to run away but he stumbled and fell to the ground. "Get away from me," he cried, picking himself up and disappearing from sight, leaving his fallen torch behind.

Finnian tutted to himself, "Strange people. Such rudeness in everyone these days" he murmured and then began climbing the tree again without looking at the boys. Soon, he was out of sight.

The boys returned to the camp, bewildered by their adventure but happy it had occurred. Bryan had lost his phone but now had a thrilling story for his grandchildren. The boys could now believe there was something better than the dull everyday life that assaulted them, and life would always seem exciting.

2.

Eight-year-old twins Cathy and Gerald were in the children's section of the town library. A place they'd been to many times before, and today they were studying some books while their mother Jill stood over them.

"Now, children," she said. "Can I rely on you both to stay here and look after each other while I go downstairs?"

"Sure, mum," Gerald said without looking up. "I always look out for my sister."

"Okay, enjoy yourself, my darlings," she replied and walked downstairs.

"Look! An Asterix," Cathy called excitedly. "I've not read this one."

"Oh, I've read them all," her brother replied and began to look around. There were three other children nearby, but in the corner sat somebody who looked out of place.

"Hey Cathy, look," he called out.

"What is it?" she said, looking at where he was pointing. Then she laughed at the odd sight of the little man, not just little but absurdly little, sitting on a cushion, apparently absorbed in a book himself. "Is he real?" she asked. "He's far too small to be a real person."

Then, both children flinched as the little man turned the page of his book while mumbling to himself. He was all dressed in green with a green top hat and ginger hair—most of it is in a thick beard. While the children stared, he stopped briefly and looked up at them.

"Don't you know it's rude to stare?" he said to them, his voice Irish and musical.

"Oh, sorry. Don't mind us," Cathy replied. "I've just never seen anyone like you before."

"That's because people who look like me tend not to show themselves very much to people."

"What an odd thing to say," answered Gerald, and his sister punched his arm.

The other children in the library, not reacting to the little man themselves, began to leave the area, leaving Cathy and Gerald alone with the newcomer.

"Oh, odd, yes. I've been called worse," he replied and then stood up to put the book he was reading back on a shelf. The children gasped at his small height—barely three feet.

"Wh. . . what book were you reading?" Cathy stammered.

"A book on Irish history, which will mean nothing to young children like you but means plenty to a five thousand year-old leprechaun."

"That's not possible," Gerald scoffed. "Nobody lives for five thousand years."

"You really think so? Well, when you get to my age, you'll realise it's possible."

The children laughed.

The leprechaun smiled and removed his hat showing a round bald head. "My name, fair ones, is Finnian Coghlan, and you don't know why I brought you here."

"What do you mean brought us here? Our mother brought us here in her car. She'll be back for us in a minute." Cathy replied.

Finnian ignored the remark and pointed to a book on the bookshelf. "Bring that book out for me, will you."

"Which book?" asked Gerald.

"The large one. The black coloured one in the middle of the shelf."

Cautiously and half suspiciously, Gerald pulled the book out. On the front was a picture of the ruined Colosseum of Rome. Both he and his sister had been past it during a holiday to Italy when they were six. It was quite heavy and Gerald had to place it quickly on the floor before he dropped it.

Finnian hopped excitedly over. "You know what this is?" he asked the puzzled children. They both shrugged. "This book," he went on, "Is a portal to another world. Another time."

"It just shows a photo of an old ruin in Italy, doesn't it?" Cathy asked, a little bored.

"Come closer" the little man whispered, now kneeling over the front of the book.

The children exchanged a look and then walked over to the little man. He held out his tiny hands to them and said. "Take my hands."

The children each took hold of the leprechaun's hands and seconds later, both heard a strange whooshing noise and the air around them filled with colours. Gasping, the twins were about to let go when suddenly they felt themselves floating in the air as if they were in the water.

"What's happening?" Cathy cried, but no sooner had she spoken. The sound and colours stopped and the three of them were no longer in the library in England but stood in a busy, bustling street.

"Good grief!" Gerald exclaimed.

The children looked around. They were standing next to the ruined building they'd seen in the picture, but now it was no ruin. It was a tall and proud construction, looking freshly built, and all around were people in peculiar dresses, all talking in a language the children couldn't understand.

Finnian laughed and said, "Toto, we're not in Kansas anymore."

The children looked at him in disbelief just as the little man was knocked to the ground by a passer-by in what looked like a toga.

"Hey, watch where you're going!" he yelled at the person, shaking his fist.

"Let's get out of this crowd," Cathy suggested, and the three of them walked over to the impressive building. There was a slight breeze bringing strange aromas of animal dung as well as food being sold by nearby vendors.

"This is ancient Rome when not so ancient," Finnian said to the children. "When gladiators fought to the death and criminals were thrown to the lions."

"Wow, how exciting!" Gerald remarked.

"All in this building behind us," Finnian went on, "Shall we see it in action?"

"Oh yes, please," the children said excitedly.

"But how do we get in?" asked Cathy.

"There are ways and means, dear little ones. Take my hands again." Finnian replied and held out his hands to them. As they did so, they were swiftly elevated from the ground, which caused yells of surprise from the people below.

"Wow, we're going up in the air!" Cathy cried in delight. "This is like the best dream ever."

The children and Finnian eventually landed on the top of the now brand-new Colosseum with its strong stone structure beneath them, and as they looked down they could see a huge crowd filling the arena while two gladiators fought with swords in the middle of it.

"Gosh, wait until I tell my friends about this!" Gerald cried happily.

After a few minutes, some members of the crowd began to nudge each other and were pointing at the strange trio above them.

"They can see us," said Gerald.

"Yes." Finnian replied. "But they can't hurt us. Maybe you'll find yourselves written into the Roman history books now."

"Can we go anywhere?" Cathy asked, her eyes dancing with delight.

"Nothing is impossible with the little people," answered Finnian. "Every dream of childhood can be fulfilled if you just believe in it."

"Oh, we believe!" the children exclaimed joyfully. "But won't our mum miss us? She might be looking for us in the library," said Gerald.

"Then we'd best get back to her." the little man replied. He clapped his hands, and the whooshing noise returned and once again, the air filled with colours. They felt as if they were falling as the blue sky of ancient Italy disappeared, but after a few seconds, the feeling was gone, and the three of them were back in the room they had just left.

"Well, that was exciting," Cathy remarked.

"I'd like to do it again," answered Gerald.

The children looked at the book on the floor with the photograph of the ruined Colosseum on the front. Cathy reached out to touch it, but it faded out of existence, leaving empty air behind.

"Hey!" she called out. "Where did the book go?"

"Finnian, I. . . ." Gerald began, but he looked around and the little man had gone. Just him and his sister looking at each other wide eyed and breathing rapidly with excitement.

"Oh, there you are," their mother called out. "I've been looking for you. Where on Earth have you been?"

"To the Colosseum of. . ." Cathy began, and then Gerald nudged her.

"To what?" their mother asked, a puzzled look on her face. Cathy gave her brother a sharp look.

"No, never mind," the little girl said, "I think we both fell asleep."

"Well, you've got school tomorrow, so I want you to be up and ready for that. Come on, we're going home."

The children had been sitting on the floor and forlornly got up to follow their mother. As they did so, something whizzed across the floor in front of them, which Gerald nearly tripped over.

"What was that?" he whispered so his mother wouldn't hear.

They both looked down at another book on the floor in front of them. It had a photo of the pyramids of Egypt on it, and as they gazed at it, they could faintly hear Finnian chuckling out of sight somewhere.

"What's this Finnian?" Cathy asked. The children's mother was now walking down the stairs.

"This is where we're going next." the voice of Finnian whispered, but Cathy and Gerald couldn't see him.

"That sounds great, but we have to go home now," the girl said. "Can you meet us here another time?"

"Another time?" Finnian asked gravely. "Believe me, children, I'll be here for all time."

Then silence and the children followed their mum out to the car. It had been a day they would never forget, and there was the promise of more exciting ones ahead.

14

3.

Lydia Asquith was looking in the mirror. It was her favourite mirror, one that had been bought at a fair in Ireland when she was ten. The old gypsy woman selling it told her parents it would bring the family good luck. They didn't believe that, and Lydia certainly didn't when her parents died ten years later, both from cancer. Now she was married, and she gingerly touched the bruise under her left eye from where James had punched her that morning. It was the classic bad marriage of a wife-beating by a controlling husband with nobody for Lydia to turn to. Her brother and sister had emigrated to Australia three years ago, leaving her at the mercy of her partner, who was convinced she was cheating on him, and although she wasn't, she knew for sure he was cheating on her.

The door to the bedroom swung open.

"I don't know why you look at yourself in that, your ugly bitch," he called out. "I'm almost glad you're cheating on me."

The door slammed shut. She cried a bit as she looked at her dishevelled light brown hair and round face in its late thirties. She had always been pretty and still was a bit. After five years of marriage, she'd been made to think of her looks a lot by her bullying husband. They got married in west London, and it was a glorious day. Only her siblings and their children were there from her side. Lydia couldn't have children and was glad she'd never have them with her awful husband, James, who wasn't bothered at all by it.

Eventually, she walked away from the mirror and sat down on the bed. It was a nice room that she worked hard to keep clean for her ungrateful husband. She'd seen the text messages from other women and she knew he stayed out late to meet them while she sat at home, alone with the TV. She was too scared to confront him over it as he was handy with his fists. Most of her friends had drifted away. When not working as a hotel cleaner, she was either alone or with him.

She slumped on the bed with a sigh and stared up at the magnolia ceiling, observing the slight cracks in it. She felt like going to sleep, but then she heard a strange noise.

"Psst!" it went.

She sat up quickly, calling out, "Who's that? James?"

"Psst! over here! Come to the mirror."

She stood up, slowly looking around. She hoped her husband wasn't playing tricks on her in case he punched her again. She looked around the room. Everything was in order. She glimpsed herself, wide-eyed and bruised, in the reflection on the wall but then saw something else in the mirror that made her freeze.

Somebody was looking at her from within it! An old man's bearded face wearing a green top hat. He was grinning at her. She screamed and put her hands to her face.

Thumping on the stairs. Her husband was coming up to check what had happened. The door burst open.

"Why are you screaming, you silly cow?" he shouted. "You're still looking at how ugly you are, I expect."

"No, James. Sorry, it was nothing," she answered.

"I'm watching the horse racing and having a drink, and I don't need you upsetting me, you gormless biddy." He slammed the door shut and thumped back down the stairs.

Lydia walked over to the mirror. It showed the bland bedroom as it always did. She looked at the reflection of the wardrobe and gasped as she saw it slowly opening by itself. She glanced around at the wardrobe behind her, but it remained shut. Looking back in the mirror the wardrobe door continued to open. She put her hands to her mouth to stop herself screaming again. In the reflection, the same little man was sitting in the wardrobe. He was all dressed in dark green and had a thick ginger beard. He looked right at her from within the mirror and put a finger to his lips.

"Don't be scared," a voice said, faint but from within the mirror. Again, she looked behind her, but the wardrobe appeared shut.

"Listen to me," the little man went on. "I want to help you."

"How?" she forced out despite her fear.

"You live with a wicked man, and I want to help you deal with him." She detected Irish in his accent.

"Really? But I love James even if he is sometimes horrible to me."

"Really, Lydia, how can you love a man like that?"

"How do you know my name?" she cried.

Before the stranger could answer, there was more thumping on the stairs, and Lydia gasped in alarm as she knew what was coming. The bedroom door opened again.

"Who the hell are you talking to? On the phone to your fancy man, are you?"

"No. . I... "

"You're not on the phone. What's the matter? You're crazy as well as ugly. Perhaps you should be sectioned if you are talking to yourself. "He turned his back as if to leave.

"You're the one who needs locking up," a voice called.

James spun round and looked at her, "What did you say?"

Her eyes wide and her hands to her face, she stammered. "No, not me. . . I. . ." she pointed to the mirror.

"You're talking to the mirror?"

"No, please, James, listen. Look in the mirror."

"What for?"

Lydia's heart was hammering. She'd never felt so scared. Her husband had beaten her before, but today, he seemed the angriest he'd ever been.

"Look in the mirror like the good lady says," came a voice in a musical Irish lilt.

"You got a boyfriend in here?" he snapped at her.

"No, please. . . I. ."

James Asquith walked over to her. She recoiled in fear, and he glanced at the mirror briefly. "There's nothing there, you dimwit."

"Come closer," a voice hissed.

"What did you say?" he snarled at Lydia. Before she could answer, something extraordinary happened. A man's fist came out of the mirror, striking James in the face. The man swore and staggered back. Lydia screamed again. She was usually worried about alerting the neighbours but this time was concerned she was going mad. James stood in front of the mirror, and a fist shot out again, striking him full in the nose. Both of them heard it crunch at the impact.

James fell to the ground, clutching his nose. A faint line of blood ran from it.

"Did you hit me, you cow?" he roared at Lydia.

"No! I did!" the voice yelled in triumph. The surface of the mirror began to ripple like water, and a tiny man leapt out from it—the man Lydia had seen in the reflection.

"Oh my God!" she screamed again.

"What is that?" James yelped as he stumbled to his feet.

"I'm not a what I'm a who," came the little man's voice as he stood in the middle of their double bed "Finnian Coghlan, the leprechaun from Ireland."

"Jeez, I'm going mad!" James shouted. Lydia shrank to a corner of the room, stumbling to her knees as she went and knocking over her bedside lamp onto the floor.

"You're a very wicked man, James Asquith, beating this good woman, and I mean to teach you a lesson."

James swore again, and before anyone could act, he picked up a pair of his wife's shoes and hurled them at the little man. Finnian didn't flinch. He caught both of the shoes in each of his hands.

"What is this craziness?" James snorted. He pulled open the wardrobe door, which he remembered had a broom in it, and he grabbed it quickly and lunged at the strange intruder. Finnian grabbed it and, with superhuman strength, pulled it out of his hands. James swore again and then yelled, "I'm calling the police."

They both heard him pounding down the stairs, and Lydia looked at Finnian while breathing in painful gulps. Her heart was still hammering.

"I told you don't be alarmed, young woman. I assure you things will turn out for the best," he said to her.

"Who on Earth are you? What are you?"

"I told you I'm a who, not a what. I am Finnian Coghlan of Glendalough and just five thousand years old, which is younger than the age of this planet is it not?"

Lydia couldn't answer and could only stare in disbelief while struggling to get her breath.

"Ironic that this beast is calling the authorities when he's been treating you so badly for so long."

"I. . . I…er guess so," she forced out.

"I mean, what can he say to the police? Excuse me, there's a leprechaun in my bedroom who punched me in the face."

"Are you a leprechaun?" she gasped, her eyes widening.

"Absolutely," he replied. "We rarely show ourselves, I admit, and when people do see us, they are rarely believed."

More thumping on the stairs. The red-faced maniac appeared in the doorway. His greying hair was tousled, his appearance dishevelled. "The police will be here soon, Lydia," he said. "They'll get rid of this weird intruder."

"What is weird. . ." Finnian cut in.

"I don't want to hear from you!" James interrupted with a roar. "Get out of my house."

"I came out of the mirror and can go back in there, you creep," Finnian answered scornfully.

"I'm seriously going mad," James groaned, putting his head in his hands.

"James, darling," Lydia called and ran to her husband. He pushed her, and she stumbled onto the bed. "But James," she went on. "I can see him, too. He says he's a leprechaun."

"Don't talk rubbish, woman. They don't exist."

That was too much for Finnian, and he leapt off the bed, grabbing the man around the neck and knocking him to the floor.

"Don't exist?!" he yelled at him. "I'll show you what someone can do who doesn't exist."

He grabbed at the bully's greying hair and yanked at it, making clumps cascade around them. Then he did a backward somersault and landed next to the wardrobe. The hair of James Asquith fluttering around the room.

James gave a wail of despair, and he got to his feet with his hands clutching at his now shiny bald head. "What have you done?" he shouted.

There was a loud knock on the door in the midst of the madness. "Aha, the police," he called in triumph and dashed down the stairs.

"I'm really sorry about him, poor Lydia," Finnian said to the shaking woman. "I'm going back to my spirit world for a moment, so he'll look like a fool when the police come in."

"But. . ." she began, but the little man instantly jumped towards the mirror and plunged into it, making it briefly ripple again like a puddle on the wall. She was once again alone in the room, looking in dismay at all the floating strands of hair that filled the air.

Voices could be heard outside and into the room came her husband with two police officers. A young man in his twenties and a slightly older woman with glasses. They looked around the untidy room.

"What did you see here?" the woman asked him.

"Where is he?" James snapped at his wife. Still shaking, she pointed at the mirror. "He went in there," she knew it sounded crazy but didn't want to lie.

"So, you're saying you saw a little man come out of the mirror," the young man asked the furious Mr Asquith. "Have you been taking drugs recently?"

"Of course not!" James bellowed. "I don't touch that filth."

"Okay, sir, just the following procedure."

"It was that mirror," he said, pointing to it, and without another word, he picked up the broom on the floor in front and swung it at the mirror, but it flew out of his hand, arced oddly in the air and struck his wife on the side of her forehead as she cowered in the corner. She screamed and put a hand to her head where a thin line of blood now trickled.

"Okay, that's quite enough," said the male officer. Through her pain, Lydia noticed that both police officers had ginger hair and Irish accents.

"He hits me all the time!" she screamed. "OH, please save me from him."

"That is enough, Mr Asquith. I would like you to come to the station with us now," the young man responded.

"But I called you to help me! There was an intruder in our house!" he yelled back at him. "Look, my hair got pulled out."

"Just calm down, sir. We just need to ask you a few questions. Come with me to the car outside, and we will discuss this further."

"Okay, Liam, you go with him. I'll stay with Mrs Asquith for a while." the lady officer said.

Cursing and protesting, James with Liam walked down the stairs, and Lydia heard the front door open and close.

"Now, Mrs Asquith, everything is under control. Please stand up, and I'll look at your head wound."

Lydia got up while the officer examined the bleeding bruise. "It's just a slight graze. I see you have another bruise under your eye. What a beast that man is. Now, if you need any further help, don't hesitate to call us."

"Thank you, Mrs. . ."

"Just call me Dolores," she answered and smiled.

"I wish my horrible husband was gone forever," she sobbed. "I hate him so much."

Dolores's smile grew broader. "I think your troubles are over," she said enigmatically and then walked down the stairs. Lydia slumped on the bed, breathing heavily as she heard the front door close a second time. After a few minutes, she nervously walked to the mirror and plucked up the courage to look at herself in it. Her hair was a mess, and she now had two angry-looking weals on her face and head. She looked at the reflection of the wardrobe, which was now closed. The grey clumps of her now bald husband's head lay at her feet. After a minute standing at the mirror there was a knock at the door. Gingerly she walked down the stairs and opened the front door. A young policeman stood there with a thick black moustache.

"Hello, is there a James Asquith here?" the man asked in a Scottish accent. "We had a call about an intruder in your house."

Lydia stared at him in surprise. "But I. . ." she paused. "I thought that. . . no, there's no intruder here." Her hands went to her face.

"Is everything all right?" he asked her.

"Yes, everything is fine," she snapped, slammed the door shut and ran back upstairs to her room.

"Oh, what is going on?" she wept as she fell to her knees. There were further knocks at the door which she did not answer.

The day became evening, and her husband had not returned. Some days, he did stay out to meet women, but he'd taken his phone with him so that she couldn't check.

The next morning was a Sunday. No phone calls or knocks on the door. She'd slept in her clothes on the bed. At about half past eleven, she ventured downstairs to make herself a coffee and some toast. She sat quietly in the kitchen when she heard something come through the door. Unusual for a Sunday. She went to the hallway and saw a single green-coloured envelope on the doormat. She picked it up and tore it open. Inside was a small white card with a handwritten message on it. YOUR WISH IS GRANTED.

She yelped, dropped it to the floor, and ran back to the kitchen.

More days passed, and she went to work as normal, but James did not come back. After a couple of weeks, she met a man at work who she began a relationship with. He was much kinder than her absent husband. Despite what James had accused her of, she'd never been unfaithful while with him. Her new man. Laurence treated her with respect. He'd been married before and was about five years older than her. One day she decided to tell him she was married and her husband had left her. He was fine with it.

Months passed with no further sign of the bullying thug. Sometimes she'd look at herself in the bedroom mirror, thinking of all the crazy things she'd seen that day but never saw such things again. Now she was finally free.

4.

Martin Barber was finishing for the day at the barber's shop he'd run for seven years. Sweeping up the hair from his last client. His business was called 'Mr Barber, the barber, ' which amused some and irritated others. It was a chilly February evening, and the night was drawing in. He was ready to go home to dinner with his wife and settle down in front of the TV. He loved Fridays as they were good for his morale. After clearing the hair away, he looked at himself in one of the mirrors and sighed. He was not a young man any more, now in his early sixties and looking forward to retiring. He'd always been in hairdressing and was pleased to be running his own business. His own hair had long gone, and he was completely bald. Plus, he'd worn glasses since he was twelve. He was hoping for a quiet and relaxing evening at home when his peace was shattered by a loud banging on the door.

"What the. . ." he exclaimed. "Who's that?"

He went to the door and pulled it open, unable to comprehend the sight that befell him when he did so.

A man burst past him into the shop, or at least he thought it was a man until he realised how absurdly tiny he was.

"Quick! Shut the door," the little man yelled in a strong Irish accent. "Seamus is after me again."

Martin took several steps back—his mouth opened and shut like a goldfish.

"Okay, I'll shut it then," the little man snapped, and he kicked the door closed himself. As he did so the barber noticed the little man was carrying something under his left arm. What looked like a grey-coloured pot with coins poking out of the top.

"He'll see us through the glass door," the little man exclaimed. "He's after my gold, the scoundrel. We'll have to hide somewhere."

"Who are you?" Martin gasped. "I'm closing for the day."

"Never mind that. This is far more important. If you help me out, I will reward you handsomely."

Then, both of them froze as a loud voice boomed from outside. "Finnian! Where are you?" it hollered.

"Who the hell was that?" said the barber.

"My rival Seamus. I'm sorry we will have to go into the spirit world for a while."

"You what?"

The little man pointed to one of the barber's mirrors. "We'll have to go in there," he said bizarrely.

"It's a flipping mirror!" Martin retorted. "What do you mean to go in there?"

"To you a mirror, but to us leprechauns a gateway to the spirit world."

"Leprechauns? Crikey, I'm dreaming."

Before Martin could say anything else, the little man, all dressed in green, grabbed his arm and pulled him over to the mirror.

"Now watch this!" he jabbered, and to Martin's incredulity, the little man and his pot disappeared into the mirror as though it was a vertical pool of water.

Before Martin could react, his eye caught a glimpse of something red outside the window in front of him. He saw another strange looking man standing outside and looking in at him with a fierce look. This man had a very long beard and was dressed entirely in red as the other one had been in green.

"You there!" he shouted at him. "Where is Finnian Coghlan?"

"Don't look at the mirror." a voice hissed from his right. Martin walked towards the little man in red: he, too, was barely three feet in height.

"What do you mean?" he asked the stranger.

"What do I mean, you half-wit?" the evil-looking little man snapped back, also with a strong Irish accent. "If you're hiding Finnian in there, I'll do terrible things to you."

Unsure if he was dreaming or hallucinating, the barber felt too scared to reply.

"Very well, I shall come in and find out," snarled the stranger. Martin took a step back, tumbling over a chair as he did so. The man in red held his hands to the glass, and it appeared to melt under his fingers.

Dragging himself to his feet, he ran to the back of the shop as the red-clad oddball stepped through the hole he'd made in the glass and walked towards him.

"Where is Finnian?" he roared.

Shaking and unnerved, Martin pointed to the back door of the shop.

"H-he w-went through there," he stammered.

"If you are lying to me, I'll turn you into a frog," the stranger growled and walked past the barber. As soon as he'd turned his back, Martin felt a hand grab the back of his neck, and a powerful force tugged him backwards. Within seconds, Martin had been pulled from the barber shop and into the spirit world.

***

Martin's head was surrounded by colours, every colour of the rainbow, and he felt like he was floating in the air. Eventually he felt himself land on solid ground, and the colours faded away.

"What the hell happened?" he exclaimed as he held his head and looked around.

He noticed the little man in green sitting on a large mushroom in front of him. His legs were crossed and his arms folded, and he studied Martin as though he were a painting in an art gallery.

"That was a close-run thing," he chirped to the bemused barber.

"It was what?" Martin answered and then saw something on his right. A square window suspended in the air, and through it, he could see the interior of his barber shop with the red clad man pacing around in it, his face like thunder. Martin looked around in astonishment. He appeared to be sitting on a large red and white mushroom himself, but it was suspended in the air. All around them, blue and green colours danced around like fireflies. Suspended in the air between Martin and the leprechaun was the pot of gold coins.

"What is happening?" Martin went on. "How is this possible?"

"I've brought us into the spirit world to escape my nemesis, Seamus O'Grady—an arrogant and cruel member of the little people. You can see him through the window. He doesn't know the powers I have or that I can use mirrors in such a way."

"This is incredible," Martin replied. "All I do is cut hair for a living. I never expected that anything like this could happen."

"You have to open your mind to such things. Please call me Finnian Coghlan. I am five thousand years old, and I come from Glendalough. I mean, you no harm. I ran into your shop to escape that evil Seamus. He's been after my gold for centuries."

Martin put his head in his hands. "I must be dreaming. Are you telling me I came to this place through an ordinary mirror?"

"Absolutely. We must stay here for a little while until it's safe to return. If Seamus sees you, he'll turn you into something."

"Like a frog?"

"Maybe. Even a beetle. He's a very powerful magician. He practiced the dark arts, and a lot of us are scared of him, so we all do our best to stay away from him."

"My wife will wonder where I am," Marin groaned, his head still in his hands.

Both of them were suddenly startled by a face appearing in the window suspended in the air next to them. Seamus was looking right at them, or so it seemed.

"Can he see us Finnian?" Martin whispered.

"No, and he can't hear us either. He knows of no way to access this plane. He's clever but not that clever."

Both sat in silence, watching intensely as Seamus stared apparently straight at them. After a few seconds, he disappeared from sight and Martin sighed with relief.

"We can't go back that way," Finnian said. "It's too risky. I'll find another way back to the human world."

"Really? How?"

At that moment Martin felt himself engulfed by a blanket of bright colours and seemed to be hurtling in the air. As a young man, he'd done a skydive, and it felt a bit like that.

"What's going on?" he called out. There was no reply, and Martin felt himself spinning in the air. He wondered if he would pass out, but eventually, the sensation stopped, and he noticed another window in the air. An oval-shaped one on his left. As he stared more closely at it he could see the interior of his bedroom in his house.

"This is my house!" he cried, and he looked around for the leprechaun.

"Indeed, it is," Finnian replied. He was hovering next to it, his arms folded. "You can get back to your house, away from wicked Seamus, by going through it."

"Louise will wonder what the hell is going on, though, if she sees me come out through a mirror. This is crazy."

"It will be more crazy if you go back to where you were before and Seamus gets hold of you. Your life would not be worth living."

Martin then noticed the door to the bedroom open, and his wife came in with a hoover. "I can't go in there now," he said to Finnian.

"Okay, maybe wait a bit. You'd scare her to death if you went in there now."

Martin looked around. It was like a dream or maybe a drug-induced trip. He appeared to be floating in the air. Below was all manner of shifting rainbow colours. Above him, everything was blue. The place was in complete silence. Finnian began to somersault in the air and moved around like he was swimming. What Martin could tell his family and friends about, he wondered, but they'd never believe him.

Eventually, Louise finished the hoovering and left the room. Finnian was watching closely and said, "Okay, the coast is clear. Back you go, Martin."

Martin drifted over towards the window then Finnian cut in. "Wait a moment. I'd promised I'd give you something in return for helping me, and so here it is." Finnian held out his hands, which Martin saw were full of gold coins. They dazzled and sparkled in the strange light.

"Wow, thanks!" Martin exclaimed and received them in his cupped hands. He estimated there were at least ten coins in there.

"Don't mention it," the little man replied and then somersaulted down into the lights below, vanishing from sight.

Martin manoeuvred himself towards the window and awkwardly pushed his head through, which was a very odd sensation, and his head emerged into the bedroom. He wondered how strange it must look as he looked around the room, which smelled of fresh flowers that his wife had placed on the bedside table. He could also still hear the hoover faintly, probably from downstairs. He began to haul himself through the mirror, dropping the gold coins onto the carpet as he did so. It was a very peculiar feeling as he dragged his body out, and he realised he'd have nothing to land on. As he wondered about it, he tumbled entirely out of the mirror and crashed loudly to the floor. He jarred his leg painfully and howled in response. To his alarm, he heard the hoover switch off and the sound of loud footsteps on the staircase. Quickly, he grabbed the fallen coins and hid them under the bed. He staggered to his feet as the bedroom door opened, and his wife stood watching him.

"Martin! I didn't hear you come in. How did you get here without me seeing you? What was that crash?"

Unable to answer, Martin laughed nervously and scratched his head. "If I told you, you wouldn't believe me," he said.

"Believe what?"

Martin couldn't give a satisfactory explanation, so he walked past his wife and went downstairs to get himself a beer from the fridge. She followed him, still asking questions that he had no answer for.

At the breakfast table the next morning, Louise was still unhappy at her husband's behaviour but he could not tell her what she wanted to know. Later Martin would collect the gold coins from under his bed. They looked and felt real, and he considered trying to sell them, but he never did. For months, he would look at the mirror at work wondering how on Earth such a strange thing could have happened, but he never saw the odd little man again. He would tell the story of it to his grandchildren when they were very small and only children. He knew they would not take it seriously.

Years later he got the gold coins valued and found they were worth many thousands, but he was a superstitious man and believed bad luck would befall him if he tried to exchange them for money. He never saw Finnian again, but once, in his barber's shop, he found a red hat left on a chair that was identical to the hat of the other strange visitor he'd had. He would dream about all this for years and wished he could explain what happened to his wife, but he knew she would think him mad. It was all his private adventure, and he would savour it for the rest of his life.

5.

Michael Watt staggered into a deserted alleyway next to the pub. He'd been drinking solidly for six hours and had left at 11:30 pm feeling sure he'd had enough. The alleyway was mostly dark, but enough light came from a nearby streetlight for him to see where he was going. Eventually he dropped to his knees, rolled onto his side and vomited over the floor. He was 48, recently divorced with a son he rarely saw. The alcohol had ended the marriage, but now he was past caring. He'd lay awake at night thinking of the purposelessness of life, and the drunken fog was all that made sense to him. He embraced his misery rather than try to fight it off. He could hear cars whizzing by outside the alley and some drunken shouting. He fumbled into his breast pocket for a pack of cigarettes and gradually sat himself up but then saw something which made him drop the crumpled box and open his mouth in astonishment. A small man, not just small but unnaturally small, stood in front of him. He was all dressed in green with a green hat and ginger beard. His tiny hands were on his hips, and he was shaking his head and tutting.

"Dear me, you're a disgrace to the human race," he said in a musical Irish voice.

"Who are you?" Michael was forced out.

"I'm Finnian Coghlan," the little man replied. "I've come to offer you redemption."

"What the f. . ," Michael began, but then he felt his mouth clamp tight by an invisible force, and his eyes widened in horror. Finnian was holding up his left hand with his index finger pointed at him.

"Now, you'll not be using obscene language in front of the little people," he scolded. "Is that understood?"

Unable to open his mouth, the drunk nodded briskly, his eyes still wide. Finnian lowered his hand, and Michael gasped and retched.

"What do you want from me?" he asked him.

"I need you to give up the booze and makeup with your family," Finnian replied.

"How?"

Finnian picked up the crumpled cigarette packet, which had two smokes left in it. He held it up in the dim light, and a golden glow seemed to envelop the box, and it turned into what looked like a lump of gold.

"Ugh this isn't real," Michael groaned, flopping to the ground, "I'm going mad and seeing visions."

"What's real is your religion of alcoholism," Finnian answered. "A lot of atheists are swallowed up by it."

"Can you blame them?" Michael moaned from the dirty alley floor. "What is the point of anything?"

"The point, my good man, or maybe not so good man, is to respect the dreams and aspirations of childhood."

"What good is that to me at my age?"

"You have a son, don't you?"

Michael sat up sharply. His eyes narrowed. "How do you know that?" he barked.

"We little people know an awful lot," he said, smiling. He handed the lump of gold to the drunk man, who eyed it suspiciously.

"This looks like gold," he said.

"Your looks do not deceive you."

"Why did you give me that?"

"So, you can sell it and pay to get yourself cleaned up."

"What do you care?"

"I care about your son."

"You don't know him!" Michael angrily yelled, staggering to his feet with the gold in his hand. "You little. . ."

Finnian held out his hand in a threatening way.

"Oh, just leave me alone," he grumbled. He looked at the small piece of gold in his hand.

"What's this worth?" he asked.

"Enough for you to change your life," Finnian replied. "Now go home. Tidy yourself up and look after the gold I gave you, and maybe you'll get more later."

"You'll give me more? I don't have a job, so I don't get a lot of money."

He gave a small smile as he examined the gold lump he held. "This is like a dream," he went on. "Will you-" but as he looked up, he saw the little man had gone. He placed the gold gingerly in his pocket and made the determined choice to go home and crash out on the sofa.

Three hours later, after spending two hours asleep, he woke with a start, having had a dream of the strange man waving his finger at him accusingly. He looked around the living room and everything was as it should be. He went to the kitchen to make a black coffee. The time was after four am, and dawn was dimly breaking. He'd placed the lump of gold, which appeared to have no distinguishing marks on it, on top of the fridge. He eyed it with disbelief. The peculiar man seemed to have turned his box of cigarettes into that, and were it not for that, he'd have dismissed the experience as a hallucination. Something he'd never had before. Not even in his pot-smoking years in his youth.

He sat on the sofa with his coffee and looked at his mobile phone next to him and at that moment it began to ring which made him jump in surprise. He picked it up and said hello and was greeted by the voice of the man in the alleyway.

"Now, have you sobered up a bit?" the little voice chirped. Michael didn't answer and flung the phone across the room, breathing heavily. He instantly regretted the decision as it smashed against the wall. How had the man gotten his number? He thought about his broken phone and decided that as he hardly ever used it, having no job or social life it didn't matter too much. It was a Sunday morning and he was looking forward to a whole day of doing nothing on his own. He picked up the TV remote and switched on the TV. His only real hobbies were drinking and watching TV. At first, he put on a news channel, but nothing on it interested him, so he decided to flick through other channels. But as he did so, he saw something on the screen which made him freeze.

The little man was on the TV, surrounded by a blank white background. He was capering about and laughing hysterically.

"Hello Michael!" he called. "Just reminding you to sober up and get back with your wife and son as soon as possible."

Mike was too dumbfounded to reply.

"We leprechauns are famous for mischief," he went on. "And there'll be terrible consequences if you don't do as I say."

A whiskey bottle lay next to the sofa, still with a fair bit of whiskey in it. Michael grabbed it and opened the lid which caused the little man to press his face right up to the screen of the TV, giving the appearance of pressing against a window.

"I advise you not to, Michael!" he said in a warning voice. "I'll be coming for you, I promise."

With that, he disappeared from the screen to be replaced by a TV advert for washing powder. Michael snapped off the TV, wheezing with shock. He replaced the lid on the whiskey bottle and slumped back on the sofa. An hour later, he was asleep.

A few hours later, bored with the TV, Michael was traipsing forlornly around his neighbourhood and saw an old drinking buddy, who he called Welsh Steve, sitting on a bench.

"All right, Steve," he greeted and sat down next to him.

"All right, Mick. How are things?"

"Not good. I'm seeing hallucinations. I've never had them before. I don't take drugs, so I don't know what's caused it. Can't be the alcohol."

"What sort of hallucinations?" Steve asked and he pulled out a brandy bottle in a paper bag.

"I get this man dressed in green talking to me about my wife and son. I've not seen them for over a year. He tells me to give up the drink and get back with them. How can I when I don't know where they are? They never phone. Sheila got custody because of my drinking, and maybe I did hit them a bit, but I can't help my addictions."

"Plus, you don't have a job?"

"Not had one for three months. Have around five hundred pounds in the bank, but that will soon go. "He reached into his coat pocket and pulled out the lump of gold. He showed it to Steve.

"This isn't a hallucination, though. The little guy gave me this. It looks like gold."

Steve examined it briefly and passed it back without much interest. "Doubt it's gold. Would be too good to be true."

"That's what I thought, but he took my box of fags and turned it into this."

Steve sniffed. "I doubt it—just some clever sleight of hand. Loads of people can do it. If anyone can do magic, why don't they do something useful like cure sick kids in hospitals?"

"Good point," Michael said, rubbing his head. "I've heard this guy on my phone and seen him on my TV."

"You need help."

"Maybe I do. I'm sure I've heard descriptions of people who look like that."

"Did he have an Irish accent?"

"Yes"

Steve laughed. "Sounds like a leprechaun."

"He said he was that, but I can't believe it."

"Some years ago, there was hysteria in America when a few people saw one in a tree."

"I didn't just see it. The thing talked to me."

Steve belched loudly, startling an old woman as she walked past. "I wouldn't worry about it. What's the worst thing that can happen?"

"I get put in a madhouse."

"At least then you'll be getting help. You're very lonely Mick. You need professional help."

"Yeah, whatever," Michael got to his feet. "I'm going home to watch TV."

"Is there anything on?"

"Don't care. I've got nothing else to do, and I fancy a drink."

"What are you having," Steve asked, taking a swig of brandy.

"Just some whiskey and maybe a bit of rum."

"Okay, see you later."

Michael walked away, looking at his lump of gold. He considered throwing it away, not believing it was gold but eventually placed it back in his coat. The wind was starting to get up. It was January, and the weather was cold. His coat wasn't really thick enough to keep it out. He got back home and staggered to his sofa, almost tripping on the fallen whiskey bottle next to it. He flicked on the TV, and an antique show began to start. He reached down for his whiskey, which had a few drops left in the bottle, and he held it to his lips. At that moment the TV changed to a blank white screen. He tried to turn the TV off, but the image remained, and then, from the left side of the screen, the strange little man appeared again.

"Oh, what?" Michael wailed.

"I told you to give up the booze, Mr Watt," the little man said. His voice coming from the TV, he wagged his finger in disapproval.

"Look, what do you care? Nobody cares about me, so why are you doing this? I don't understand."

The little man disappeared off to the left of the screen for a few seconds and then reappeared, holding the hand of a child who Michael instantly recognised. His eight-year-old son Gavin. He hadn't seen him for a year but instantly knew it was him." What are you doing?" he shouted at the TV. "How are you there with my son?"

Gavin started crying. His brown hair was dishevelled, and he looked to be wearing pyjamas as if he'd just been spirited out of bed.

"Dad!" he wailed.

"How is this possible?" Michael yelled again and dropped his bottle of whiskey on the floor, which spilt out onto the filthy carpet, but Michael was too alarmed to care.

"Give up the booze, you wretch!" Finnian shouted, and there was a flash of rainbow-coloured light on the screen, which then went black.

Michael sank to his knees and then lay flat out, face down on the carpet. He couldn't take any more of this and decided he'd admit himself to a psychiatric ward at the hospital first thing Monday morning.

***

The doctor's name was Sayeed Ahmed, and he seemed sympathetic and understanding of Michael Watt's plight.

"So, you've not taken cannabis since you were 19," he was saying after five minutes of conversation.

"Correct, sir," Michael answered, his eyes downcast with shame. He knew he smelled of booze as he'd not bathed for four days. He just didn't care anymore. He was at the end of his tether.

"Now you say this small man had an Irish accent. Did he tell you his name?"

"Finnian Coghlan." was the reply. The doctor was writing notes as he answered. "And did you have any religious thoughts?"

"Not really. I don't believe in any religion."

"Okay, good," the doctor scribbled on. "So, your hallucinations began Saturday evening and gradually got worse on Sunday. Do you have any next of kin we can contact?"

"My parents are dead. My wife and son left me. I have nobody," he replied, consumed with what he felt was justifiable self-pity.

"It's very sad," the doctor replied. "And you don't have a job?"

"No."

"Okay, I think it's best we keep you in the ward for a few days on medication, and we'll see how your illness progresses. If you have further hallucinations, please let us know immediately."

"Okay, thank you, doctor," he replied sheepishly. The doctor led him to a small room in the ward and asked if he had a toothbrush or washing supplies. Michael had the presence of mind to bring a few such essentials in a small bag as well as pyjamas. As they stood outside the room, an old woman ran towards them, flailing her hands.

"Jesus is coming. Jesus is coming!" she cried and carried on down the corridor.

"Okay, have some rest, Mr Watt and if you need any help don't hesitate to tell the nurse available. Dinner will be at six pm every evening."

"Thank you, doctor," he repeated and slumped onto his bed. There was a small wash basin in his room and a toilet just outside it. No TV in his room, so he realised he'd get bored very quickly. There was a TV in the communal room outside where he saw patients and nurses watching it, but not being able to choose what he wanted to watch, he decided not to join them. After half an hour, a nurse came into his room, a petite Indian woman.

"Your medication is at eight pm," she said.

He nodded in response, and she left the room.

"Oh, what a mess," he wailed, crashing down on his pillow, which was as hard as the bed itself.

"All a mess because you won't listen to me, Mick Watt." a familiar voice called from the corner of the room.

Michael sat up as if shot and looked in the corner. The little man was there again, grinning profusely. Michael dashed for the door and kicked it open.

"Nurse!" he screamed. "I can see him again."

A middle-aged male nurse ran to him and came into the room. They both looked around, but nobody was there.

"He was there!" Michael yelled, pointing at the corner now vacant.

"Okay, calm down, Mr Watt," the nurse replied. He had a Scottish accent and a wispy beard. "When the medication takes effect, the visions should begin to lessen. It is probably best that you have your first tablet now. It is called olanzapine and will help with the hallucinations."

"Okay, clear off now then," Michael retorted, flailing his arm. "Nothing can help me. I'm better off dead."

"You need to calm down and let the medication take effect," said the nurse, leaving the room. The door swung shut, and Michael sat down on the bed. A few minutes later, the nurse returned with a small plastic beaker of water and a tablet in another tiny beaker. Michael took the medication, thanked the nurse and lay back on his bed. He fell asleep and missed his dinner which nobody told him about, but he needed the sleep and woke up late into the night. At around eleven o'clock, he tried to leave the room, but the night nurses, a couple of stocky men sitting outside, hissed at him to go back to sleep. He was wide awake and terrified, and in annoyance, he lashed out at one of the nurses. The big man avoided his fist and grabbed the man in an armlock before marching him back to his room.

"Look, you need to sleep," the nurse said. "Don't disturb the other patients."

"But I'm lonely and terrified," Michael wailed. "Please help me."

"You can talk to someone in the morning."

So, Michael slumped back on his bed and waited, wide awake all night, for the dawn.

Dawn eventually arrived and Michael was allowed to leave his room and help himself to porridge for breakfast. The other patients ignored him, to his relief, as he didn't need their problems as well as his own. He then returned to his room and endured an insufferably dull few hours before Dr Ahmed knocked on the door. Michael opened the door to him, seeing him smiling broadly, showing clean white teeth.

"I have a nice surprise for you. Follow me."

Michael followed the doctor out of the ward and down some stairs to a waiting room. Standing in the waiting room were his ex-wife and son.

"Daddy," Gavin called and ran to embrace him.

"Oh, Gavin, how I've missed you," he said and looked up at the boy's mother who had a small smile but otherwise was showing no emotion. She was wearing a long red coat and had her greying hair in a bun.

"I want to be a good dad, Gavin," he babbled happily. "I'll give up the drink and see you more often."

"Can daddy come back with us, please?" he looked up at the doctor, his eyes imploring.

"Maybe in a couple of days. He's had a very bad time and needs to recover," the doctor replied.

"But I'm recovered now doctor," he said and gave the surprised doctor a hug.

"You are not seeing visions and having strange thoughts?" he asked Michael.

Michael took a step back and did a salute to him. "Fine and ship shape. Seeing my son has cured me."

"So, what's been happening, Mike?" his ex-wife asked coldly. "A nurse called up and told us about your problems. Gavin was heartbroken, so we had to see you."

"How did they find you?"

"Your next-door neighbour has our number and has been growing concerned. He said you'd been saying strange things to Steve."

"Oh," Mike paused. "So, he contacted the hospital."

"Yes." and she stood up and turned her back to him. "I don't want you back with me. I can't forgive you, but Gavin deserves to see his dad. Don't you agree?"

"Absolutely," Mike answered, grinning at his son, who clapped with joy.

"The little man was right, Mum," Gavin cried happily.

Michael's grin vanished.

"What little man?"

Gavin didn't notice the gravity of his father's voice.

"A tiny man in green appeared in the garden and said you wanted to see us."

Michael recoiled and took a step back, "Was his name Finnian?"

"Yes. Finnian Coghlan."

Michael gasped, and Sheila spun around to look at him. "Something wrong?" she demanded.

"Did you see this little man?" he asked her.

"Why no, I was angry at Gavin for talking to strangers. I told him not to do it again."

Michael stood in silence for a few seconds.

"Oh, but never mind that. We're back together now, and I promise I'll be a better man. I'll get a job and stop drinking. Please, believe me, Sheila, I've been so lonely."

"Oh, don't wallow in self-pity. That's what split us up."

"Mum!" Gavin yelled.

"I'm sorry, Gavin, but you don't know what it was like. If Daddy wants to see you more often, he can, but we'll never be together again, okay?"

Gavin sighed, nodded and looked down.

Later, Michael went back to his room, and his son and ex-wife went home. He'd be spending a few more days in the hospital. Coffee-making facilities were in the ward and he began to make himself one, vaguely aware of the mirror in front of him that showed what a sorry figure he was. His face was bloated and unshaven. His grey eyes were puffy. His bald head showed signs of his alcoholism, with bulging veins all over it. He lifted the coffee to his lips while looking in the mirror into his own eyes when a movement in the mirror caught his attention. He jumped in surprise, making coffee spill down his shirt. The little man was in the reflection, standing on the floor behind him. Michael looked around but saw nobody, then looked back in the mirror, and Finnian was still there. The little man had a gentle smile on his face and gave him the thumbs up.

"Keep it up, Mick," he called happily and then disappeared.

6.

Nine-year-old Kenneth Ridley enjoyed visiting the Scottish Highlands. His parents would set up a picnic, and he'd wander off to look for small animals or watch birds. On this occasion, on a hot August afternoon in the school holidays, his parents had come across another married couple who were old friends of theirs. Being an only child, he did not want to listen to their dull adult conversations. His parents, Richard and Heidi sat on the grass with the couple, whose names he didn't know and didn't really care about and were talking about house prices and other things that didn't interest him. His parents gave him a mobile phone to keep in touch, told him not to wander too far, and he walked away alone. The last time he visited the highlands, he was certain he saw a weasel, but it ran away too quickly for him to be certain.

The heat sapped at him, and he found an old cave to shelter in for a few minutes. He had a satchel on his back with several bottles of water in it. He sat down on a stone at the cave's entrance and drank gratefully from one of them.

The view was amazing. He wished he could share it with someone else, particularly someone his own age. The green hills stretched all around for miles. He could see birds of prey circling around. That sort of thing excited the boy. After several minutes of resting, Ken got up to leave when he heard voices from inside the cave. It sounded like two people talking from somewhere further in. He wondered if he could spy on them without them seeing him. He wasn't supposed to get involved with strangers. He tiptoed further into the cave, looking carefully around. It was dark at the back of the cave and he wondered how far it extended into the hillside. His parents wouldn't want him to get lost. That would really upset them. His eyes began to adjust to the dim light, and as he strained to see more, he was aware of what looked like two tiny men working on some odd-looking contraption full of glass bottles and connected with tubes. It bubbled and hissed like some kind of experiment. Ken crouched behind a rock and tried to make out what was going on.

"Brian O'Reilly, I've been distilling poitin' for three hundred years. I know what I'm doing," the voice came from one of the little men. All dressed in green clothes with a green top hat and with a thick ginger coloured beard.

"Finnian, you'd still be making people go blind if you didn't listen to how I did it," the other man replied. This one was clean-shaven and also all in green with a green hat. He looked younger than the other one.

"You know it's legal now, Brian. That's because people learned to make it how I make it."

Both men had Irish accents and looked barely three feet in height. Suddenly, Ken slipped on a pebble, which rolled over to the two odd men.

"What's that?" Brian asked, looking towards him. Ken held his breath, his heart hammering so hard he was sure the strange men would hear it.

"Probably just a bird, Brian," Finnian replied after a few seconds. "Now, where were we? Oh yes. I'm sure it's ready to taste now."

Overcoming his fear, Ken peeped out from his rock, seeing the two little men drinking some clear liquid from small glasses.

"Tastes perfect!" Finnian cried in delight. "The finest poitin you'll ever drink."

Ken then sneezed and, in alarm, tried to shrink back into a dark corner.

"That was no bird, Finnian," Brian said in his distinctive Irish brogue. "Someone is watching us."

Ken gasped and got into a defensive crouching position. He could hear footsteps coming towards him.

"Okay. you little scamp," a voice said next to him. "Who are you and what are you doing?"

Ken looked up to see the two little men standing over him. Their faces were not cruel, but their eyes were accusing. They each held a glass of the drink they'd been making.

"Don't hurt me," Ken pleaded. "I just got curious about who was in here."

"We won't hurt you, little boy," the bearded Finnian said.

Suddenly, Ken's phone rang, making the two strangers leap in surprise.

"Don't worry, it's only my parents," Ken said, and he spoke to his mum for a couple of minutes, saying he was OK and sitting in a nearby cave.

"Amazing technology, Finnian," Brian said. "We've been around for thousands of years and never seen anything like that before."

"How have you been around for thousands of years?" Ken asked curiously, overcoming his initial fear.

"Well, Brian is a youngster at three thousand, and I'm over five thousand," Finnian said matter of factly. " We leprechauns live a long time."

"Leprechauns!" Ken exclaimed. "Is that what you are?"

"Indeed, we are," Brian said. "We haven't got any gold on us right now if that is what you were expecting."

"I don't want gold," Ken said. "I just want adventure."

"Like stories of smugglers and pirates, I suppose," Finnian answered. "Well, we're not that, but we can grant wishes."

"Shall we grant this boy three wishes, Finnian?" Brian asked, taking a big swig of his drink.

"Well, he's not having our poitin, Brian. It's not suitable for children."

The two men walked away to their odd distilling machine and began to extract more drink from it. Then they sat down to sip more on some flat rocks.

"Can you really grant three wishes?" Ken asked, walking over to them. "I mean, like anything in the world."

"Only if we're not too drunk, Ken," Finnian said with a laugh.

"You know my name as well?"

"We know the names of all the important children," Brian cut in.

"Am I important then?"

"Too many questions kid. Just ask for your three wishes," Finnian said nonchalantly, his voice slightly slurred by drink so it seemed.

"In that case!" Kenneth said excitedly. "I wish that all wars would end all over the world."

Finnian yawned and then clicked his fingers. "Wish granted," he said.

"What?" Ken exclaimed. "You mean all wars are now over?"

"Well, yes, unless you wish them back again," Brian replied.

"No way!" Ken cried. "I wish climate change would be reversed right now."

Brian clicked his fingers. "All done, little boy."

"Really!" Ken shouted excitedly

"You have one wish left, Kenneth, so choose wisely," Finnian said seriously.

Ken was silent for a while, unable to comprehend what was going on. Then his face lit up, and he said. "I wish I could live forever."

Finnian yawned again and clicked his fingers. "Done, my friend, but you'll regret your third wish."

"Really?" Ken asked, puzzled. "Why is that?"

"I'm five thousand years old and have seen hundreds of people I loved grow old and die, and the grief can be indescribable, not to mention the many moments of boredom. It will be a tough burden, I'm sorry to say."

Ken scratched his chin nervously. "Really?"

"We leprechauns are immortal, Ken," Brian said. "We will never die, and so you'll have us for company, but every ordinary human you ever know will die before your eyes. It will be a sad and lonely experience. Thankfully, for Finnian and I, we have access to our poitin. You didn't wish to be a child forever, which may have made it more bearable for you, but you will become an adult and everyone you fall in love with as an adult will disappear in front of you."

"Oh," Ken was silent. "But all wars will end and climate change will be reversed?"

"You did some good there, kid," Finnian said with a laugh. "Just a shame you'll have an eternity of boredom to go with it."

"How do I know my wishes have come true?"

"If you put on the news, you'll hear that all war has ended, and scientists will tell you that global warming is no longer happening," Brian said, taking a swig of poitin.

"And as you'll never die, don't bother trying to kill yourself," Finnian laughed and clinked glasses with Brian.

"I can't believe what you're saying. Surely you are both mad," Ken retorted and walked out of the cave to the sound of the little men's drunken laughter. Ken strode indignantly down to where his parents sat on a blanket. The other couple had left.

"Where have you been?" his dad asked. "Fancy a sandwich?"

"Yes, thanks, Dad," Ken replied, taking the cheese and tomato sandwich offered to him. He sat down quietly.

"You look bothered by something," his mother said. "Have you been speaking to strangers?"

"No," he lied. "I just felt bored on my own."

"Well, don't wander off on your own then," his dad said. "We are going home in a minute."

"Have all the wars ended?" he blurted out to his parents.

"What?" they both said.

"No, never mind. Yes, I want to go home. I'm tired."

Ken sat silently as his dad drove him home to their house in Edinburgh. They were not originally from Scotland but his dad had moved them there for his work. He'd been born in London and had moved at age six. He'd made some friends but still got bullied for various reasons. Mostly, he stayed alone playing computer games.

The heat was sweltering, and when Ken got home he ran straight for the fridge to drink some chilled apple juice from a tall carton. All the time, he was thinking of the strange little men in the cave. He wanted to put the TV news on to see if all wars had ended, but his mum had told him to go straight to bed. With his strange thoughts as well as the heat, he couldn't sleep a wink. He wondered if he really would live forever and what kind of experience it would be.

The next day, at breakfast, Ken's dad said something interesting. "Did you hear, Heidi, that a lot of countries have announced that they'll be dismantling all their nuclear bombs?"

"Really?" she said, only half interested.

"And many militant groups in Africa have said they'll stop fighting each other."

"I don't believe that," she replied.

Ken listened without comment. He ate several mouthfuls of toast and jam and then asked to be excused. Once he had done so, he dashed into the living room to put on the news channel. Then, before his eyes, he saw images of several world leaders announcing an end to hostilities against neighbouring countries. He leapt in delight, pointing and laughing at the TV screen. He watched for half an hour, hoping climate change would also be mentioned, but it wasn't. Maybe too soon.

Had the leprechaun's wishes come true? If so, he would live forever as well, but he didn't want to put that to the test. He was still scared of the situation and did not really know how powerful Brian and Finnian were. He wanted to go back to the cave but suspected it would be hard to find. He really wanted to see the little men again. Today was a Wednesday, and it was a school holiday. He didn't have close friends to see but also felt too excited to sit in front of a computer game. What should he do?

✳✳✳

Years passed and all world conflict had ended, or so it seemed. Even north Korea had dismantled its nuclear arsenal. Scientists were commenting on climate change, saying they believed the measures to tackle it were really working.

All the time, Ken thought about the two strange little men and what they'd done. He went to university and got a degree in law, and everyone he spoke to there was delighted that people had stopped fighting each other. However, he hadn't put everything right, and when he was in his twenties, his father died suddenly from a heart attack aged fifty-one. Several years later, his mother also passed away from cancer. Driving home from his mother's funeral, he was now twenty-nine and lived alone. He'd had a few girlfriends, but nothing serious as they'd all regarded him as a bit odd. It was a sunny August day, like the day when he'd met the two little men. It didn't feel as hot as most August days, so perhaps climate change really was reversing. He sat in a chair in his back garden in Edinburgh. Once his parent's house, but now his. He'd poured himself a beer, and he leaned back with his eyes closed. Then, he heard a voice.

"Kenneth Ridley, young man! How are you?"

He sat up with a start and saw the two leprechauns standing in front of him. They looked exactly as they had on that day twenty years ago. They were both smiling sweetly.

"You guys again," he exclaimed. "After all this time and after my poor mother has just died, you turn up."

"Yes, we're very sorry about that. You didn't wish eternal life for your parents, but we have ended all wars and reversed climate change as you wished us to. "Finnian said.

"I noticed," Ken answered, "I got no thanks for it."

"We shouldn't have done it, Ken. We were in a merry mood with the drink when you saw us as a boy in that cave," said Brian.

"You're saying you wish you hadn't granted me three wishes?"

"We're very powerful, as you have now noticed. I think we were hasty. We like to impress children and we went too far," Finnian said.

The two little men sat on two empty chairs opposite Ken in the back garden. Their little legs dangling high above the ground.

"We think you'll regret living forever, and we came to apologise. We can't undo the wishes despite the good you have done for others," Brian said. "Seeing everyone you ever loved pass away is a lonely experience. There are several of us immortals. Obviously, we can keep you company but you may tire of us."

"I was in a car crash when I was twenty-three," Ken cut in. "Two of my friends died, and I got out without a scratch. Was that because of you?"

"I'm afraid so, my lad," Finnian said sadly. "You will live to be old, and then you'll be old forever like us."

"I wish I could have stayed as a child. Everything was so much easier then," Ken replied.

"Yes, Brian and I were far too merry on the poitin that day. You may have seen on the news that people still die in awful ways, but not through wars as you wished them to end."

"So, what happens now?" Ken asked wearily.

"Try to forget about us. Try to forget a lot of things, as memories can haunt you forever. The sun will engulf the Earth in billions of years, but we'll still be here, as will you be, but in a different realm of existence. I'm sure we'll see you around, so keep your chin up," Brian said.

Ken put his face in his hands. He didn't know how to respond. After a few seconds, he looked up, and the little men were gone.

7.

Ted Betts was in his garden shed. He'd been very busy that spring planting flowers and vegetables in his back garden in Essex. He had no clue about the extraordinary situation that was about to befall him. He cared for his wife Liz, who was seventy-nine and confined to a wheelchair. They did a lot of charity fundraising for local schools and hospices. On that sunny day in May, Ted was looking for his gardening gloves that he had misplaced. He found them in a dark corner next to a spider's web. Picking them up carefully so as not to disturb the spider, he left the shed and began to walk to the back door of his house. As he did so, a clear and shrill voice pierced the silence.

"Sure, and begorrah, you're a lovely man, Ted Betts, so you are."

Ted stopped and slowly looked around. He could not believe what he was seeing, leaning against his garden shed was a tiny man, barely three feet in height and all dressed in green with a green hat. He had a ginger beard that he was ruffling slightly.

"Goodness me!" Ted exclaimed. "Who are you?"

"My name is Finnian Coghlan, a young man and I'm going to change your life."

"I'm not young. I'm seventy-nine. How did you get in here?"

"Young compared to me. I'm five thousand years old."

Ted stood stock still. He dropped the gloves he was holding and stared silently in disbelief. His mouth had gone very dry. "You look like a leprechaun," he said. "I never thought such things existed."

"It seems as though such things do. Now, I'll cut to the chase. I'm going to give you something that will change your life."

"In what way?" Ted replied. He realised he was shaking at the appearance of this mysterious stranger.

Finnian walked towards him and instantly Ted took a few steps back.

"There's no need to be afraid, Ted. I came to give you these."

The little man held out his right hand, and Ted saw what looked like several plant seeds on his palm—a palm with numerous lines in it like the rings of an ancient tree.

Nervously, Ted edged forward. The man was barely higher than Ted's knees. "What are they?" he asked.

"Seeds to a very special type of plant. A plant I want you to grow in your garden."

"Really?" Ted replied. His fear was beginning to subside. "Can I look at them?" The seeds were placed in Ted's hand, and he looked at them for several seconds.

"I've never seen seeds like this. They're all gold-coloured."

"To grow a golden plant," Finnian replied with a grin.

"Okay. I'll plant them in the garden later. First, I have to get some food for my wife as it's lunchtime."

Finnian tipped his hat. "Yes, you're a very good man, Ted Betts, and I'm going to change everything for you with my powers."

Ted laughed nervously. "How did you know my name?"

"I know the names of all the good people. Now attend to your wife, then plant the seeds, and I'll visit you again later."

"Okay. I. . ." Ted realised he was speechless. He walked to his patio door and opened it with his free left hand. The right-hand carries the seeds. He glanced over his shoulder and the leprechaun had gone. The garden was surrounded by high walls, and Ted had no idea how he could have gone so quickly. He looked down at the gold seeds in his hand. There were five of them, and they looked like small pearls. Were it not for that, he'd have thought he was dreaming.

He went to his kitchen, placed the seeds in an empty tea cup and began preparing his wife's lunch. She was watching TV in the living room in the chair she'd had for four years, as her bones had weakened severely in recent years. Now she couldn't walk at all. He prepared her favourite, beans on toast. It wouldn't take long, but he wouldn't tell her about the strange visitor. Such a revelation could have a bad effect.

Eventually, lunch was ready, and he brought it to her. As they were both retired and not very mobile, they watched a lot of TV. As ever, Liz was glued to it.

"Here you are, Liz," Ted said, placing the lunch on a table in front of her. She wheeled over and began to eat. Ted sat down in a nearby armchair, thinking about what had happened in the garden. As a child, he'd loved fairy stories, but he was long past the age of believing any of those things were real. He watched his wife as she chewed her food and then had a glance at the newspaper next to him. He saw nothing much of interest, and gradually, he dozed off.

The scream woke him up instantly, and he almost fell out of his chair. As he got used to his surroundings, he looked around for the source of the noise, and then he saw something that would remain with him forever.

It was the little man, Finnian Coghlan, who was in the room with them, but what really got his attention was his wife, who had screamed. Her wheelchair was on its side, its wheels spinning, and she lay on the floor, flailing her arms. Ted leapt up immediately causing a slight pain in his chest as he did so.

"What's happening?" he yelled.

Finnian was reaching out for Liz's hands. "Get up, my lady. Get up," he said repeatedly.

"What have you done to her?" Ted shouted in alarm.

"Just watch this, my good man." Finnian cried, and he grabbed Liz's hands and made a leap in the air that was not humanly possible. Liz was pulled into the air with him, and she was on her feet. Ted reached out to stop her falling while Finnian appeared to be floating in the air. He let go of the lady's hands, and she didn't fall to the ground. She stood in front of her husband, Ted, her blue eyes wide with terror, and she looked down at her feet. She took a step backwards and realised she didn't need the wheelchair. She could walk.

"Ted," she gasped, "I'm not going to fall. I can walk again."

Ted reached out and grabbed his wife's shoulders. Neither of them was looking at Finnian, who was balanced on the top of a nearby cabinet. Liz was taking deep breaths and trying not to faint. She hadn't walked properly for five years.

"It's a miracle," she whispered as she pushed Ted gently out of the way and began to pace slowly around the room.

"Now you know what the little people can do," came the shrill Irish voice.

Ted and Liz both looked at him, their hearts racing.

"Did you do this?" Ted asked him. "How?"

"How indeed," Finnian replied nonchalantly and dropped off the cabinet onto the floor. "I said I'm going to change your lives. This is my first miracle, and you'll see my second one when you plant those seeds I gave you."

Ted was dumbfounded. He stared into his wife's eyes, who stared into his. Surely, things like this weren't possible. "Well, thank you," he said.

"Yes," Liz added, taking a few more ginger steps around the living room. "This is amazing. My legs feel strong again."

"Was a delight to be of service to you good people. Now, I'll be off, and I will see you around." He strolled over to the kitchen, his tiny shoes skittering on the vinyl floor. They watched him go in silent disbelief. A few seconds later, he came back in and said, "Don't forget to plant the seeds," and he ran out again.

Ted looked at his wife. They were both shaking. "Can you really walk now, Liz?" he asked her.

"He touched my hands and I felt an energy pulse through me, and my wheelchair tipped over. I got up and my legs supported me, feeling strong again."

"It is truly a miracle," he said, shaking his head. "Shall we tell the local paper?"

"It's surely too good to be true. Maybe it's just a temporary thing," she replied.

"He gave me these peculiar seeds. Gold coloured. I've never seen seeds like it. I left them in the kitchen."

"Well, go and plant them, Ted, like the little magician said."

"I don't believe in leprechauns. This sort of thing doesn't happen in real life. The only thing that helps people is money. Not anything supernatural like what is happening with us. Liz, could this be some kind of collective dream?"

"I'm wide awake, Ted, I can assure you, and I can walk now, which is wonderful."

She sat down in an armchair and began to cry. Ted reached out to comfort her in an embrace and stayed there for over a minute. As her crying subsided, Ted walked to the kitchen to get the golden seeds.

"What do you think will happen when I plant them?" he asked.

She smiled through her tears and got up excitedly. "Let's find out," she said.

They both walked quickly into the garden. The sun was shining. The birds were singing, and the breeze was gentle on that perfect day in late spring.

Ted walked to the back of the garden, near where most of his flowers were and found a patch of earth in the corner undisturbed. He scraped back the soil with a trowel and placed the seeds in the ground. Then he covered them over and took a few steps back.

"I sense something will happen, Ted!" Liz called in delighted anticipation. "Like that energy that made me walk again."

She was not wrong. Barely a minute later, they could both hear a faint rumbling noise, like a train going by but deep underground. The ground shook, and Ted walked to his wife and held her arm nervously.

Something burst from the ground, shooting up six feet high in about ten seconds. It was a huge gold-coloured plant with leaves and branches thickening around it.

"It's beautiful," Liz gasped.

Ted was speechless. In his seventy-nine years, he'd never experienced anything like what was happening today. After a few minutes, the incredible plant stopped growing, and a huge leaf formed at the front of it, about five feet in height. As they gazed in awe, it became like a mirror, and they could see their reflections in it. They stared in silence as it began to mist over, and the likeness of a tall young man emerged in front of them. Both Ted and Liz leapt in surprise as they recognised their son Martin, who had died thirty years ago in a car crash aged just twenty-seven. Their eyes locked with his, and they could see extreme sadness in his face. He was dressed exactly as they last saw him in a clean white shirt and jeans.

"Martin!" Ted exclaimed. "Is that you?"

"Indeed, it is," came a familiar voice near the ground on their right, and Finnian Coghlan came strolling over to them, looking content.

"It's a gateway to the spirit world, but the living and the spirit cannot exist on the same plane, don't you know? You can't go there, and they can't come here. If you go there, you can never return here."

"Dad," a faint voice called as if from the end of a long echoey tunnel. It was the voice of Martin, their long-dead son. "Mum," he added.

"Yes, Martin, it's me," she called in delight. "Can you really see us how we can see you?"

"It's all very faint," he said, "I can see you vaguely."

Ted looked at Finnian. "Can we reach in and touch him?" he asked, his heart hammering.

"Very risky," Finnian replied. "Once you get pulled in, you're gone. Maybe it's best not to reach in. I can't promise you can come back."

Ted looked at his wife, who was still shaking, and back at the leprechaun. "You made my wife walk. That sort of miracle never happens ever, not even to good people. Yes, we are good people, like you said, but if things like this happened, it would be all over the news in an instant."

"So now you believe in the little people," Finnian said with a grin.

"I believe in evidence. Liz and I have always been humanists but with an open mind to the possibility of things like this. What else can you do?"

"Oh, all sorts. I thought it would be nice to give somebody a treat with it being such a lovely day. I get lonely being five thousand years old and seeing so many generations live and die in front of me."

As he spoke, the image of Liz and Ted's son began to fade away, and the huge golden plant began to wither and collapse to the ground.

"So, you're telling us there's an afterlife?" Liz asked the little man. "And this is what you showed us today?"

"I'm telling you the spirit world exists, good lady. There's nothing to fear from life or death. If you know where to look, then anything is possible. I guess I've done my good deed for the day. I don't show myself to many people, so think yourself privileged that I chose you for this experience. I performed a miracle so you could walk again, but the spirit world takes us all eventually, no matter what our circumstances are."

"So where will you go now?" Ted asked.

"My business is mainly with children. They have to believe in me more, but good adults like yourselves sometimes get my attention. I'll be leaving you now. I've done something very special for you but you won't live forever in the physical world. Don't be afraid because good words and deeds bring about their own rewards, and if you keep living the good life, then anything is possible."

He tipped his hat to them, began to whistle and then vanished in a flash of rainbow-coloured light.

8.

The adventures of Finnian Coghlan, the leprechaun.

13-year-old Edwin Luckhurst looked with dismay at his school report as he left class for the last time that summer. Low grades and negative teacher remarks. The worry was not what he thought about it but instead the reaction of his demanding stepfather who had only the highest standards for him. He had a short temper, and both Edwin and his younger brother lived in fear of him. Forlornly, he walked home alone, just a ten-minute journey from his school, and he tried to think of ways that he could explain himself.

His phone rang in his pocket, and he had a brief conversation with his mother over what he was having for dinner Fish and chips! His favourite.

It was a warm day with a gentle breeze, and he thought about calling friends to play football that evening, but it depended on his stepdad, who might ground him for his bad report. He'd been married to Edwin's mum for five years after his real dad left him for another woman. Him and his brother Anthony rarely saw him now, but he was a selfish man, and they didn't miss him, but his stepfather was not a suitable replacement.

He reached his house and opened the door of the terraced abode with his key. His tiny chihuahua ran to greet him, barking happily. Edwin grinned and gave the dog a stroke.

"Mum!" he called out. "I'm home."

His mother, Sandra, appeared from the kitchen.

"Oh, hello, love," she said. "Your dad is out at the moment. He's looking forward to seeing your school report."

Edwin gulped. "Okay, whatever," he said, hanging up his school bag.

Later that evening, after a shower and dinner, his stepfather Keith arrived home. He smelled slightly of alcohol and had been in the nearby pub most of the day, having had a day off work to use up his annual leave from the car factory where he was employed.

"Hello, Ed," he called to him. "Where's Anthony?"

His brother was at a friend's house playing computer games. He'd gone straight out as soon as he'd arrived from school.

"He's out."

"OK. I'll have my dinner and see your school report."

"All right then," was all he could think of, and he shakily went to his room to ponder what course of action to take should the worst happen. It seems Anthony's report didn't matter, as he was only ten. Maybe with Edwin being 13 and adulthood looming, it was a more pressing concern. He sat nervously on his bed, looking at his report. Opposite him was a full-length mirror, and he could see himself shaking with nerves. After a few minutes, his mother entered. She was a kind woman but rarely intervened with her husband's rages out of fear of him. Both Edwin and Anthony wondered why she ever married him.

"Hello Edwin," she said with a smile.

"Hi, mum," he answered nervously, his report in his shaking hands—no higher grade than a D for any of his subjects. The teachers commented on his apathy and laziness. His attendance was poor as well as he often skipped classes out of sheer boredom. Things could really kick off soon.

"Mum, I'm scared," he said.

"Why's that darling?" she asked, sitting next to him with an arm around his shoulder.

"My report's really bad. I'm worried about how angry he'll be."

"Oh, he'll be okay," she replied, looking at herself in the mirror next to her son. She was a short woman with blonde hair in a pigtail. They both looked at their reflections for a while and then they heard the man's footsteps coming up the stairs.

"What will I do, mum?" he asked, almost crying.

She looked at his report and tutted.

"Oh dear, this isn't good, Ed," she said, shaking her head.

The door swung open to the bedroom. Keith stood there looking at them, his greying hair frizzy and his grey eyes gazing at them intensely. He was developing a beer belly. Edwin hoped he wasn't drunk.

"Moment of truth, Ed," he said. "Hand it over."

"Okay, Dad," he said nervously, holding out the shuddering piece of paper.

His mum smiled and got up. "I'll leave you boys to it," she said and left the room. Edwin listened to her retreating footsteps while her husband focused on the report closely.

For about thirty seconds complete silence, and his face did not change as he stared at the teacher's notes. Then, the inevitable happened.

"This is not good Ed," he said. "Not good at all."

"I'm sorry, I. . ."

"You should be sorry. This is disgraceful. How dare you behave so poorly in school. I thought I was raising you better than this."

"Well, I. . ."

"I suppose you've got some excuse, have you?" he cut in. Then he picked up one of his brother's toy cars from the dressing table and threw it at Edwin. Edwin gasped and deflected the object with his hand, retreating slowly away.

"You know what I think of lazy children?" he said, his voice lowering, which it did when he was angry.

"Mum!" Edwin called out in terror.

His stepdad left the room, and Edwin heard him go to his parent's room and he knew what was happening. He was going to get the slipper. He'd been hit by it before a few times during the man's rages. What could he do? He glanced around the room in alarm, wondering how he could escape his fate, when he heard a voice he'd never heard before.

"Psst over here," it went. It seemed to be coming from the mirror. It was a mirror they'd had all his life. He wandered over to it, wondering how a voice could have come from it. As he neared it, something extraordinary happened. Two small hands protruded from the glass and grabbed his arms. The hands pulled him towards the mirror, and Edwin braced himself for a painful impact against it, but instead, he felt nothing, and everything around him went black.

"What's happening?" Edwin cried in alarm just as his stepfather returned to his room with a large brown slipper to beat him with. Edwin looked around and realised he was not in his bedroom any more. He was in a place that surely only existed in dreams.

He was surrounded by darkness, with points of orange light darting around him. A faint sound of music seemed to be playing, and then he noticed someone in front of him. A tiny man in a green suit hovered in front of him, his arms folded. He had a thick ginger-coloured beard and piercing eyes that were as green as his suit.

"I'll tell you what's happening, young Edwin. I'm getting you away from that cruel beast."

Edwin was stunned into silence, and then he looked behind him and saw a large rectangle the size of his bedroom mirror. He could see the inside of his room where his stepfather was opening the wardrobe and looking under his bed. He couldn't hear him but could see his face was twisted with rage. He seemed to mouth the words. "Where are you?" and then disappeared from view.

Edwin looked back at the tiny man. "How has this happened?" he asked him. "Who are you?"

"I'm Finnian Coghlan, the leprechaun," the little man said. His voice was musical and Irish. "I grant favours to people all over the world when the fancy takes me. Today, I've decided to help you. I'm going to turn the tables on that beastly man."

Edwin stared at him, stunned. "Really? How?"

"Within the spirit world, everything is possible," he answered.

"The what world?" Edwin answered incredulously. "Have I come here through my mirror? I must be dreaming."

"You've come into the spirit world. All mirrors allow it. Just like how the human brain is a portal to another world. How else could a human being have an afterlife?"

"Is there an afterlife?"

"You'll find out one day."

"Why not tell me now?"

"Aren't your dreams telling you enough?"

Edwin was silent. He looked back at his dimly lit bedroom. His stepfather had gone, but now his mother was in the room, and she, too, was looking in the wardrobe and under the bed. She looked hysterical, and Edwin reached his hand out towards the opening, but Finnian slapped his hand away.

"Don't do that," he said. "Don't let them see you."

"But my mum. . ."

"She'll be fine. Don't worry about her."

"What are you going to do with me?"

"I like to help children in distress."

"I'm not a child. I'm thirteen."

"Thirteen, not a child?"

"I was at my grandparent's house last weekend and I was looking at a book of children's stories. My grandad said I was getting too old for them."

"You're never too old to believe in the little people."

"Are you really a leprechaun?"

"Yes. A very old one. I've been around for thousands of years, travelling the world in search of excitement and to help those in need."

"That's amazing," Edwin replied. "My brother will never believe this."

"Your brother isn't being terrorised by a vicious man. That's why I came to you and not him."

"He is a horrible man. Always drinking and shouting at us. My mum is too scared to leave him."

Finnian sighed, "Yes, so much of life is governed by fear."

"So, how will you help us?" Edwin asked, still incredulous.

Finnian cleared his throat and looked upwards. "Within the spirit world, there are all manner of inhabitants. I have many friends who are fantastical and powerful. I'll get one of them to go into your world and confront that apology for a man."

"Oh," said Edwin, scratching his head. His movements felt different in this new realm, like movements in a dream. "So, you won't go and confront him yourself?"

"I have a much better plan," the small visitor said with a wink. "My friend Elwira will know just what to do."

"What do you want me to do?" Edwin asked, noticing the dancing lights around his head changing colour. He could see nothing else in the darkness, only the odd little man. He wasn't even standing up on anything. It seemed as if they were both hovering in the air.

"I want you to go back into your room, but do it quietly so you won't be noticed for a while. Then I want you to go downstairs and lure that man into your room."

"They'll be wondering where I disappeared to. They might have called the police."

"No, they think you climbed out of your window and are hiding outside."

"How do you know that?"

Finnian tapped his nose thoughtfully and winked again. "We little people just know," he said.

"Okay," said Edwin, and he walked or seemed to drift towards the rectangle that showed him his room. "So, I just go in there, do I?"

"Yes, go ahead. I'll be waiting for you. Don't worry, my lad. I aim to help you."

"Thanks," Edwin replied nervously and reached a hand out towards his room. As soon as his hand touched what felt like a warm wall of water he felt himself tumbling forward and was pulled, as if by gravity, back into his room.

***

"What the. . ." he exclaimed, and he looked around. His room was empty but he could hear voices and thumping footsteps downstairs. He noticed the voice of his brother.

"I haven't seen him!" Anthony yelled out, and his dog barked as if in agreement.

"Well, where is he?" shouted the bully, and Edwin was alarmed to hear the sound of breaking glass or crockery. Gingerly, Edwin stepped out of his room and didn't look back at the mirror. Quietly, he stood on the landing.

"Keith, what have you done with my son?" he heard his mother wail, tears pricked his eyes at the concern in her voice. "I'm going to my mother's for a couple of hours, and if he's not here when I get back, I'm calling the police."

"Oh, shut up, Sandra. He can't have gone far. He's not clever enough."

Edwin heard the front door slam and his mother's shoes tapping down the stone garden path. He was relieved his mother wouldn't face more aggression from that scary man.

"Anthony, look in the garden again. I'll check upstairs," the man boomed.

Edwin stood at the top of the stairs. He wondered if he should confront the bully or try and hide in his room. He knew there weren't good places to hide unless he went back into his mirror. He still wondered if that had been a dream or some kind of hallucination, but he didn't have time to think for long as his stepdad began pounding up the stairs. Instead of returning to his room, Edwin ran into the bathroom and cowered in the bathtub. He crouched there, shaking as he heard the brute reach the top of the staircase.

"Okay, you little wimp. Where are you?"

"I'm in here," a voice called. Edwin gasped. The voice had come from his room! Seconds later, he heard his stepfather slam the door open and step into his room. The floorboards creaked under his weight.

Then, something very odd. Complete silence. A silence that seemed unnatural, and after a couple of minutes, Edwin stepped out of the bathtub and walked towards his closed bedroom door. He stared at it for a while, looking at the drawing of a fire engine his brother had stuck on it a few weeks ago. After a few seconds, he faintly called out, "Dad…"

No answer. Shakily, he reached for the door and pushed it open. What he saw was a sight that would stay with him for the rest of his life.

The whole room was festooned with giant webbing, like that of a spider, and in the middle of the room, he saw his stepfather entangled and currently motionless with his eyes closed.

Edwin gasped and then looked up at the ceiling. A large spider, bigger than any he'd seen before, clung there. It was over three feet in length and completely black with a red skull-like mark on its abdomen. Looking back at the entangled man, he realised he had fainted. He knew that his stepfather was terrified of spiders, and it seemed his fear had made him pass out. As Edwin gazed in astonishment at this scene a movement to his left caught his eye, and from the mirror, emerging as if it was a vertical pool of water which rippled slightly came the little man in green. He stood and looked at Edwin, his face grim.

"Hello again, young fella," he said.

Edwin stared at him, speechless with shock. The spider twitched its legs, sending a chill down Edwin's spine. He, too, was a little scared of spiders.

"Elwira has done a good job, don't you think?" Finnian asked the boy. "Trussed him up good."

"Is he unconscious?" Edwin asked, his lips trembling as he spoke.

"Yes, he will wake in a little while, and I'll put him in his place, don't you worry."

They stood in silence as Keith Luckhurst began to regain consciousness. He groaned and strained at the webbing encircling his entire body.

"Okay. Elwira, you can go now," the leprechaun said and Edwin shuddered as the spider scurried over to the mirror and disappeared into it. It was a terrifying sight and one that would surely forever haunt his dreams.

"Wakey wakey, you big bully," Finnian called out. He went to the bathroom and came back with a beaker of water, which he threw over the man's face.

The man spluttered and pulled himself out of his slumped position. He looked at the two figures who regarded him closely.

"What the hell happened?" he called to them.

"Not nice, is it?" the little man went on, his face like thunder. "To be trapped and in fear."

Still wrestling with the sticky webbing, he didn't reply. Edwin stood close to the door where the webbing couldn't reach him. He noticed the large slipper on the floor next to the bully, which he'd clearly intended to beat him with.

"Edwin, where were you hiding?" he hissed.

"Never mind that," the leprechaun cut in. "I want you to learn the error of your ways and leave this lad alone."

"Where's that spider?" the trussed man asked.

"In a better place," Finnian answered.

"I've never seen a spider like that," he went on. "That's the most terrifying thing I've ever seen."

"So now you know how this lad feels when you threaten him with violence." said the leprechaun, his stern face almost becoming a smirk.

"Can you let him go now, Finnian," Edwin asked. "I think he's learned his lesson."

"Well, have you?" Finnian cut in, "Because if you haven't, I can make so many other unpleasant things happen to you."

"Okay, yes," the man jabbered. "I'm sorry, Edwin. Can you please now get me out of here."

Finnian shrugged. He reached above his head and clapped his hands. At that moment, a blinding flash of light filled the room, and the room seemed to shake a little, which made Edwin stumble to the floor, and he landed face down on the carpet. Groaning, he pulled himself upright and looked around. The spider webbing had all gone and his stepfather was in front of him on his knees and mumbling incoherently to himself.

"What the hell happened Edwin?" he asked, now no longer seeming like the bully.

"I think we've been visited by a leprechaun," Edwin answered, laughing nervously.

"When such a thing exists, I might agree with you," was his answer as he struggled to his feet, looking at his wide-eyed face in the mirror.

Edwin cautiously walked to the mirror and put his hand out onto the glass. It was cool and hard, as it should be. Maybe this had all been a dream after all. Then, they both stopped still as a sound filled the air. It was coming from the direction of the mirror and sounded very much like laughter. Edwin rubbed his eyes and shook his head in disbelief.

"Whatever it was, Dad, he seemed to enjoy playing with us," he said.

After a few minutes of silence, the two people left the room and Edwin never heard his school report mentioned ever again.

9.

The adventures of Finnian Coghlan, the Glendalough leprechaun

It was a Sunday afternoon on a winter's day in the house of 74-year-old widow Liz Holter. She was sitting reading a book in her living room when she heard her cat Chester come in through the cat flap. He bounded over to her and leapt onto her lap, purring softly.

"Be careful, Chester," she said. "I almost dropped my book."

She was so engrossed in her book that she didn't hear the cat flap rattle a second time and hear the footsteps scurry across the floor.

"Are you hungry, Chester?" she said, putting her book aside. The cat just stared into her eyes. "Okay. I will get you a bowl of meat."

She slowly got up, and Chester followed the old lady as she shuffled into the kitchen. Asleep in his basket by the fridge was her pet spaniel, Rex. Also, in the kitchen was the other visitor she was so far unaware of. Slowly, she reached for the door to the kitchen cupboard, where she kept the cat's food. She first removed the cat's bowl and placed it in the corner of the kitchen.

"How are you, my good lady?" a voice chirped from behind her.

"Good Heavens! Who's that?" she exclaimed, almost stumbling over. A little man then stepped into view. A man of such short height, it was impossible to believe. He was all dressed in green with a green top hat and had a ginger coloured beard.

"I'm Finnian Coghlan, the leprechaun," he added.

"How did you get in my house?" she gasped. She was shaking with surprise and alarm.

"Don't be afraid of me, Elizabeth," he went on.

"You know my name as well?"

"Oh, I know all sorts of things," he added, smiling. "Every now and then, I'll visit a mortal like yourself and surprise and entertain them."

"You certainly surprised me," she said. "What do you want from me? I hope you don't want money."

Finnian laughed. "OH, I've got all the money I'll ever need. Haven't you heard of our reputation for hoarding gold?"

The old lady was silent. She was still shaking. Chester looked up at her. Rex stayed asleep.

"My cat is hungry. I was getting him a tin of meat," she said.

"How did you know he was hungry?" the little man asked. He had a strong Irish accent she noticed.

"Well, I. . ." she began, but he interrupted.

"Why not ask him?"

" What do you mean, ask him? Are you mad?"

"Witches have cats," he went on. "Usually black ones, not black and white like him."

"I'm not a witch," she replied, starting to get annoyed at this odd intruder.

"Of course, you're not," he answered. "But you have a talking cat."

"A what?"

At that moment, the strange figure pulled a handful of gold-coloured dust from his breast pocket and sprinkled it over her cat. The cat spluttered and recoiled.

"What are you doing?" the lady cried in dismay.

"Didn't you see what he was doing?" a voice replied.

"Who said that?" she yelped.

"Not me," laughed Finnian.

They both looked at the cat. He was still pawing at his face as the dust settled around him.

"Aren't you getting me my food, woman?" said the voice, a thin and reedy voice. The old lady's eyes widened.

"It's you talking, Chester!" she almost screamed. "I have a talking cat!"

At that moment, the man in green fell over to the ground, shaking with laughter. He was holding his belly, and his hat fell off, exposing a shiny bald head.

"Goodness me!" she said. "I must be dreaming."

Her dog suddenly sprang awake. He looked around at the odd scene.

"I suppose you're hungry too," the cat seemed to say. Its mouth moved strangely as the words formed.

Finnian stopped laughing. He reached into his coat again and threw another handful of gold-coloured dust over the dog. "Well, answer then," he shouted, chuckling as he did so.

The dog sneezed and shook its head and then began barking, but then the bark became a loud, deep voice. "What is going on here?" it said. "Who woke me up?"

The cat and dog looked at each other. Their eyes are alert with a newfound intelligence.

"Who cares about your sleep? I want my food," the cat said.

"Oh, what is happening?" the old lady cried, her hands flew to her face.

The cat and dog both looked at her. Finnian Coghlan picked up his fallen hat and placed it on his head. "I told you, Mrs Holter," the little man said. "I visit people to surprise and entertain them.

"Are you trying to give me a heart attack?" she answered. "I've never been so shocked."

The cat and dog then looked at Finnian. "What are you doing to our beloved owner?" the dog asked gruffly. "Don't scare her. She needs us."

"And I need my food," the cat added. "I get most of it from her."

Finnian folded his arms and looked thoughtfully at the two animals. "Millions of people have pets like you," he said, "But they can't talk to them. I've given you that opportunity, so don't have a go at me."

"You strange man," the lady said. "I ought to call the police."

"What will you tell them?" the little man replied, turning to her. "Excuse me, but a leprechaun has got into my house and caused my pets to talk? I don't think they'll take you seriously."

At that moment, there was a loud knock on the front door. "That's my daughter and grandson," she said to him. "They can help me deal with this madness."

Finnian sighed. "Whatever," and he shrugged nonchalantly. The two animals looked at him as she shuffled out of the kitchen. A few seconds later, she returned with her relatives.

"Is something happening, mum?" her daughter asked.

"I'm going mad, Louise. A little man calling himself a leprechaun threw dust over Chester and Rex and made them talk."

Louise and her twelve-year-old son George looked around the kitchen. They saw both animals looking alertly at them. Finnian had gone.

"Everything seems okay, Nan," George said.

"Of course, it's okay. She makes such a fuss," came a voice. The dog's mouth moved as the words appeared. The voice seemed to come from him.

"What the. . ." Louise exclaimed.

"I told you! Something unbelievable has happened!" Liz shrieked.

"Calm down, mum," her daughter said, putting a comforting hand on her shoulder. "There's got to be a rational reason for this."

"What isn't rational is how hungry I am," the cat wailed. Its mouth salivated as it formed the words.

The twelve-year-old boy shouted in disbelief and ran out of the room. He thumped up the stairs, passed his nan's stairlift and stared into the bathroom mirror, panting hard. He looked at himself in the reflection, his brown curly hair shaking, his brown eyes wide.

"What did I just see?" he mouthed to himself in incredulity. He stayed there for a full minute when he noticed another face in the reflection next to him. At first, he thought his mum had followed, but then he saw the green hat and ginger beard.

"You saw leprechaun miracles, my lad," his voice said to the startled boy.

George whirled around. He saw nothing. He looked back at the mirror. No strange little man. Eventually, he began trundling back down the stairs. He saw his nan sitting in the living room armchair, her hands shaking as she held a glass of brandy. His mum was standing next to her, one hand on her shoulder. The two animals had stayed in the kitchen.

"I saw something in the mirror, Mum," the boy exclaimed. "An old man."

"Did he have green clothes and a beard?" his nan replied.

"Yes."

"That's him."

Then, the three family members flinched as the two animals walked into the living room side by side.

"You're not going to talk again, are you, Rex?" asked their shaken owner. "Or you, Chester?"

The cat meowed softly. The dog barked.

"Oh, thank goodness they're back to normal," she gasped.

"If there's a strange man in your house, you need to call the police, Mum," her daughter said. "You saw him in the bathroom, George?"

"It's no good, Louise, he's a leprechaun," Liz went on. "I know it sounds crazy, but. . ."

"There's no such thing, nan. I'm twelve now, and I don't believe in anything like that now."

"But you've seen him, and I have as well."

The three people looked at each other in silence. The two pets slunk back to the kitchen. George followed them and reached down to pick up the cat. He held it up in front of him and looked at it intensely.

"Go on, talk," he said, but the cat just rolled its eyes. Eventually, the boy put the cat down and went back to his relatives.

"Maybe we were all hallucinating," he said to them. "The cat doesn't talk now."

The boy's nan just stared at him, her hands still quivering as she held her glass of brandy. Then, there was a sharp knock on the front door, which interrupted the silence. George jumped and said. "I'll answer it."

He walked through the hallway and opened the door. What he saw made his jaw drop in astonishment. Another tiny man stood in front of him, also dressed in green, but this one clean shaven with dark, greying hair under a top hat.

"Good day to you, young sir," he chirped happily. "I wonder if you've seen my friend recently. I saw him walking in the direction of this house."

George stared at this visitor, his mouth dry. He, too, was barely three feet tall, and he stammered to him, "D-does he has a ginger beard?"

"Yes, that's him!" he replied in delight. "He stole some of my magic gold dust, and I hope he's not been up to any mischief with it like enchanting animals, which it can do". He paused. "You didn't see him in a mirror, did you?"

"Well, yes,"

"Ah, he's run off into the spirit world, the cheeky scamp," he replied, shaking his head. "Okay. Thanks for your time. I'll be off now."

With that, he turned and walked away up the garden path.

George closed the door, his face pale, and walked back to his mum and nan.

"Who was it, George?" his mum asked. "You look like you've seen a ghost."

"Not a ghost mum. I think I saw a leprechaun."

Footsteps could then be heard from the staircase, and another little figure came into view. "You didn't see a leprechaun," he said, smiling. "You saw two leprechauns. Good day to you now," and the bearded Finnian Coghlan scurried out through the cat flap, whistling with joy.

The Mysterious Reflection
Reflection in the Mirror

10.

The adventures of Finnian the leprechaun 2

It was a sunny spring day in north London, and the staff at the bank were seeing their customers as usual. There was no suggestion of anything untoward happening, but unfortunately, on that day for the bank and its customers, something would begin to unfold, which everyone became aware of as the bank queue began to get quite heavy on that Friday afternoon.

Three men entered the bank, all wearing black balaclavas and each holding a shotgun. As they entered, a grey-haired, middle-aged woman in the queue saw them and screamed. At the sound of her, several others looked around as the man leading the trio, also the tallest, held up his gun and pointed it at them.

"Everybody on the floor!" he shouted. "Face down. Now!"

Gasping and crying, the dozen or so people queuing did as they were told. Two serving staff members of the bank stood in silent shock behind their stations.

"You two as well!" the man shouted. He had a distinct Scottish accent. "Out here and down on the ground."

With their hands up, the terrified man and woman walked over to the other customers and got down slowly. Another armed man grabbed the male banker's shoulder, an Indian man with Saju Deb written on his badge.

"You!" he shouted, hauling him off his knees. "Take us to the safe."

"Okay, s-sir," he stammered in response and was ushered at gunpoint to the back.

"Somebody helps us," a young, overweight man gasped on the floor.

"You say something?" one of the robbers yelled, this one with a Midlands accent.

"No sir," he replied.

"Give me your wallet."

"Oh, okay."

"Take what you want, just please don't hurt us," wept a young black woman.

"Do as you are told, and you won't get hurt," he shouted back.

There had been heavy rain all morning, but now the sun was out, and through the bank window, a rainbow was visible. Nobody took any notice of the two small dark shapes that seemed to be gliding over the rainbow and were moving in their direction.

"Now open the safe, and don't try anything!" the Scotsman yelled at the petrified Indian.

"Okay, sir," he replied

While engaged with this in silence, the door to the bank opened, and two people came in. Everyone was too preoccupied to notice them, but after a few seconds, one of the robbers caught sight of them and whirled around to them, pointing his gun.

"Goodness me, Brian!" one of the visitors exclaimed. "We come off a rainbow to be greeted by a scene like this."

One of the women saw the new arrivals and screamed again. Two tiny men in green clothes and wearing green top hats were surveying the scene. One had a thick ginger beard, and the other was clean-shaven, but both had green twinkling eyes.

"Get on the floor!" the nearest robber yelled. He pointed his shotgun at them.

The two men, both barely three feet tall, stood unmoved.

"What will you do if we don't?" the clean-shaven visitor said, his Irish accent, "Are you scared of these people, Finnian?"

"I've been around too long to be scared of anything, Brian," his companion replied.

The gun went off. A woman screamed, and passers-by outside looked up.

"You idiot!" the Scottish robber shouted at the shooter.

"Yes, You idiot," answered Finnian. He then held up something between his fingers that looked like a bullet. "Were you looking for this?" he asked.

"We've gotta get out of here." said the robber by the safe. He bundled some notes into a sack and ran towards the door.

"Nobody is going anywhere," answered Finnian. "You need to learn that if you want money, you should be prepared for honest toil like everyone else."

One robber tried to push past the two little men, but one of them grabbed his ankle and, with superhuman strength, hurled him across the floor, and more screams from the prone bank customers erupted.

"You can all get up now!" Brian shouted. "The leprechauns are saving the day."

The fallen robber dragged himself up and fired his gun again at the two strange men. Again, they remained unmoved. More screams erupted, and then Brian shook his head and spat something into his hand.

"I caught this one in my teeth, Finnian," he said, chuckling.

"How wonderful it is to be indestructible, Brian" was his reply.

The three robbers ran for the door and Brian took off his hat and pulled something out from within it. At first, it appeared to those watching like a long black shoelace. But it expanded quickly, and Brian hurled it at the armed trio. It enveloped them as it grew, and then it flew upwards towards the ceiling of the bank, and now the three villains were trapped within, cursing and shouting.

Crying and screaming, the customers all got to their feet, staring upwards in amazement at the sight of the three intruders suspended helplessly above in large black netting.

Finnian reached his tiny hand out to his friend Brian, who shook it enthusiastically.

"A job well done, I think," Finnian said to him.

"What would they do without us?" he replied. They were both smiling broadly.

"Who are you guys?" the Indian bank worker asked. "How did you do that?"

"Us leprechauns are pursuers of truth and justice despite our reputations for being selfish and obsessed with gold," said the bearded Finnian. "We came to help you today. Not everyone is so lucky."

"But people like you don't exist." said the female bank worker, a ginger-haired woman in her 40s." You must be actors."

"Can actors do that?" Brian laughed, pointing to the black netting suspended from the ceiling holding its three writhing captives.

"Anyway, I'm calling the police," said Saju, bringing out his mobile phone. "When they see the CCTV, they won't believe it."

"Haha, you can't catch us on film, m'lad," replied Finnian. "That's why so many people don't believe in our existence."

The young, overweight man was filming them on his phone as they spoke. "I'll get you on film," he said.

"Well, good luck with that fella," answered Brian. "Finnian, shall we get on our rainbow again?"

"It's still there, Brian. Absolutely. Our good deed for the day is done."

The two little men walked towards the bank's exit while the shocked bank customers and staff watched in silent disbelief.

"Good day to you people," said Finnian, turning and raising his hat briefly. "But we've got a rainbow to catch. Maybe we'll see you in Ireland."

They exited the doorway and walked out onto the busy street, then they exchanged a few words and Finnian walked back in, "I almost forgot something," he said, reaching into his coat pocket, and he hurled what looked like gold coins into the bank.

"Here's some compensation for you. Don't spend it all at once." Laughing, the little man rejoined his friend outside, and they walked away.

Still in stunned silence, the people in the bank watched as they suddenly disappeared and two tiny specks then appeared on the rainbow and flew out of sight.

"Nobody will believe this," said the young man, looking at his phone. "So, I've got it on film."

Several people gathered around him to look at his phone, but all they saw was a blank white screen.

"You haven't got anything," said another young man.

"I thought I did," he replied in annoyance.

A lady picked up one of the fallen gold coins on the floor. "At least they gave us this," she said. "Real leprechaun gold."

Saju came over and looked at the coin. "There's about thirty of them all over the floor," he said. "What a crazy day."

At that moment, the rainbow disappeared, and the sun shone brighter. It truly had been a crazy day.

11.

The adventures of Finnian the leprechaun 3

"What to adults is fantasy, to children is the truth?" Finnian slurred the words as he said them, affected by a whole bottle of poitin he'd drunk over that day, but it was his birthday, so why shouldn't he?

"Aye, I guess so," replied his friend Brian, also slightly intoxicated.

They were sitting on the top of a brewery in Dublin. It was Finnian's 5001st birthday, or so he thought, as it was impossible to remember after so many of them. It was high summer in late June, and the sun was baking down.

"What better way to spend your birthday, Finnian?" said Brian. "Drinking the finest drink in the finest city."

"Absolutely," he replied, and he belched loudly. "I just wish we didn't have to acknowledge the calendar of that wretched man Julius

Caesar. Truly an evil tyrant, if ever there was one like most of those ghastly emperors."

"There's been plenty of tyrants since then, Finnian, but yes, he was one of the worst."

"I told you time and time again the people of Gaul wanted to live in peace until that beast brought his hordes in. Even Jesus paid respects to him. Render unto Caesar what is Caesars and blah blah blah."

Brian yawned, stood up and staggered slightly before sitting down again. "I suppose you'll be wanting your present my buddy," he said.

"There's no rush, but I guess I'd like to get something. You're not 5001 every day."

"I'm about 3015. I've lost count as well."

"I never met Caesar, but if I had, I'd have given him what for," Finnian went on.

"It's too late now, my friend. The brute has come and gone. We can't airbrush history but only learn from it."

Finnian hauled himself to his feet and placed his emptied bottle of poitín on the floor. "Okay. Brian, my buddy," he said, "Where's my present?"

Brian chuckled, and stumbling over to the corner of the roof of the Guinness depot, he brought out an object from behind an old barrel.

"Here you go, my friend," he said, grinning and holding it out to him. "Genuine Aztec gold."

"Aztec gold!" Finnian exclaimed.

"Yes, I was in a mountainous area of Mexico recently and found this in a cave."

Finnian took the object and looked at it. It was shaped like a raft and had what looked like four golden people on it. It shone in the summer sun.

"It looks like that famous Colombian raft in a museum," he said. "I'm sure it isn't, but it looks like gold to me, and I'll be thanking you, Brian, my buddy."

Brian tipped his hat and grinned broadly. His teeth shone in the light.

"So where do we go now?" he added. "In over 5000 years, I've been everywhere in the world, and I suppose only outer space is left."

"Maybe we could hitch a ride on a rocket and go there ourselves," Brian said, laughing at the idea.

"I'm sure we will one day, but I've had too much to drink to consider it right now."

Brian yawned again and then gasped as he looked out over the city. Finnian leapt slightly and then looked out to see what Brian had seen.

In the distance, a rainbow had appeared which was odd as there had been no rain in Dublin for over a week.

"That's not right, Brian," Finnian said nervously. "Something is amiss."

As they watched the rainbow, they saw a small dark speck moving across it. It moved very swiftly and seemed to be moving towards them.

"I think I know what's happening, Finnian. I think it's Seamus."

"Seamus O'Grady!" Finnian exclaimed, horrified. "He is after the gold you gave me."

Seconds later, the speck became clearer, and it landed in front of them on the roof. It was a little man in a red suit, his face contorted with rage. Someone both Brian and Finnian hated, and he hated them.

"I'll not be wishing you a happy birthday, Finnian!" he cried, his accent an even deeper Irish than theirs. "Being 10, 000 years old, I'm your elder and better. There's no living thing on Earth older or better than me."

"What do you want, Seamus?" Finnian asked.

"To be honest, I want to be rid of you forever. I'm the most important leprechaun in the world."

Brian laughed. "Important? You mean children like you more than us?"

"Children, as well as adults, don't believe in us, so that's an absurd comment. I don't care what anyone believes, but I'll be taking that gold off you right now."

"And how do you plan to get it?" Finnian replied, and without another word he hurled the empty bottle at Seamus that had been at his feet.

"Bah!" Seamus exclaimed, leaping away to the side as the bottle smashed on the floor behind him. "Throwing a bottle. Is that all you've got?"

"Let's get out of here Finnian," Brian said and grabbed his friend's arm. He walked him over to the edge of the roof and leapt off, holding Finnian tight.

"Whoa!" Finnian cried as they landed feet-first in a deserted alley next to the building. "I nearly dropped your present."

A cat wailed and darted in front of them as they ran out into the street.

"Out of the way, Felix!" Brian yelled, "I've got to help my friend."

"Perhaps we ought to escape into the spirit world." Finnian said, gasping. "Can you see a mirror nearby?"

They stopped and looked around. The street was busy, but nobody was looking at them. They had the power of invisibility but didn't always use it as it required a lot of energy.

"I can see you both!" a voice cried from above. "I'll find you and take what I want."

At that moment, a car passed carrying a trailer of potted plants. The flowers wobbled as they passed. That's when they realised their opportunity.

"Get onto there, Brian," Finnian yelled, and the two green-suited friends leapt onto the trailer, landing face first in soil.

"Urgh!" Finnian exclaimed, spitting mud out of his beard.

"If we keep our heads down maybe Seamus won't see us," spluttered Brian, also with a face full of mud.

The car rolled on, and the two leprechauns didn't look back.

After about ten minutes of the journey, Finnian cautiously peered over the edge of the trailer. They were on a motorway, and he recognised the road as one that led to Dublin Airport. There was no sign of Seamus.

"I think we lost him, Brian," he said. "I reckon we should hitch a ride on a plane to make completely sure we've got away from him."

"Not a bad idea, Finnian. I doubt you've had a birthday like this before."

Finnian laughed and then groaned and held his head. "Maybe not, but I've drunk this much poitin before on such a day. Now I've got a splitting headache."

"Worrying about what Seamus will do to us if he catches us as well. Do you remember what happened to Paddy?"

"Oh, aye, Paddy McCormick," Finnian replied thoughtfully. "One of my best friends and Seamus caught hold of him and accused him of trying to steal his stash of plundered gold about two hundred years ago. I've not seen or heard from him since."

The car was slowing down and peeping over the side. The two leprechauns saw that it had stopped at a petrol station.

"I think we can get off here, Brian," said the older leprechaun. "We're not far from the airport."

Tentatively, the two little men jumped over the side of the car's trailer and scurried away to a grass verge, still looking around nervously for their pursuer.

"We seem to have lost him, Brian," Finnian whispered.

"He looked pretty mad, though. I don't think he will give up for a while."

A plane could be seen nearby, landing at Dublin airport. Without further delay the two friends scampered towards the direction that they'd seen it. Dashing across roads, they eventually reached the side of the airport runway.

"Which plane do we take, Brian?" Finnian hissed.

"The first one we see take off, I'm guessing, and. . . wait! Look!"

Finnian looked and gasped. They saw the red-suited Seamus walking along the side of the runway. Even from over fifty yards, they could see his face was like thunder. His unnaturally long beard fluttered in the breeze.

"Quick the hedgerow!" Finnian exclaimed. They departed into bushes, staring intently at the ancient leprechaun who hadn't seen them, or so they hoped.

They watched for several minutes as Seamus stood stock-still on the runway, staring ahead of him. Then something unusual happened. A tall young man was walking over to him, clearly unhappy and gesticulating with his hands. He looked like a member of the airport staff. Seamus was watching him impassively and seemed to be in a heated conversation with this young man. The conversation went on for a minute or two, and then there was a flash of light from them, which made the two watchers' recoil. When they looked back, the young man had gone, and Seamus appeared to be holding something in his hands, which he hurled to the side of the runway. It was small and green and was moving by itself.

"Goodness, Brian!" Finnian exclaimed. "The scoundrel turned him into a frog."

"Maybe that's what happened to Paddy," Brian wheezed uneasily.

"Let's get away from here before he sees us."

Brian and Finnian, as silently as they could, darted out of the hedgerow. Leaving the airport, they saw an old lady talking to a taxi driver, and the car's back door was open.

"I tried this once in New York," Finnian whispered. "Get into the back."

Out of sight the two little men jumped into the open car and covered themselves with a blanket that was on the back seat.

"Thank you, driver," they heard the old lady say. "I'll sit in the front with you."

Inwardly the leprechauns sighed with relief as the doors were closed and the car started. They heard a murmured conversation between the driver and his passenger but couldn't make out what was said. The journey seemed very long, and they wondered if they'd end up in Belfast, but eventually, the car stopped, and the driver got out, as did his passenger. Peeping out from the blanket, Brian saw that they'd stopped outside a large detached house. He saw the old lady talking on a mobile phone while the driver smoked a vape."

"Let's get out of here," he whispered to Finnian. "Quick while their backs are turned."

Opening the back door, the two figures ran out unseen into another thick hedge.

"I wonder where we are, Brian," said Finnian, their eyes darting around.

"Somewhere in Ireland, no doubt," he replied.

The two little friends walked alongside busy roads and eventually found themselves walking over a green field, at which point Finnian slapped a hand to his forehead and cried in amazement. "I know where we are! I'm back at my birthplace in Glendalough."

"How appropriate for your birthday, Finnian," answered his friend. They walked over the lush grass to a small graveyard and stood by the tall stone tower within it.

"None of this was here when I was born, as I pretty much predate most human activity in this area," said Finnian. He was still holding the golden raft Brian had given him for his birthday. With all their recent escapades, somehow, he'd managed to cling hold to it.

"I was born by the side of the lake," he went on. "Let's visit it."

"Okay, buddy."

There were a few tourists around but none of them took any notice of the two leprechauns. Sometimes they were invisible, but sometimes they weren't. After a few minutes, they reached the lake, and both little men saw a young woman on her knees by the side of the water. She looked like she was praying.

"I wonder if that's your fairy mother," Brian said with a laugh. "She's certainly pretty enough."

As the two figures neared, she turned to look at them, and then she stood up and smiled.

"Finnian!" she called. "You've come back to your birthplace. Come closer so I can give you your birthday present."

"Are you my mother?" Finnian asked. "It's so long since I last saw her I can't remember what she looked like."

She was dressed in a long white silken robe. Her hands reached out as if to embrace her son.

"What's that you've got?" she asked, looking at the golden raft.

"Oh, just some Aztec gold my friend gave me recently. He thought it would make a good present."

"Let's see it," she said, and Finnian placed it in her hands.

"Aha!" she cried and stepped back a few steps. "I tricked you!"

A blast of light exploded in front of them, causing the two friends to stumble to the floor. When the light vanished, they saw Seamus O'Grady, his eyes flashing with delight and a wild grin on his face as he held aloft the golden object.

"Damn you, Seamus!" yelled Finnian. "What did you do that for?"

"I've got your gold," he replied with a sneer. "Now, I could turn you into a frog like I did Paddy McCormick many years ago, but I wouldn't want to ruin your birthday now, would I?"

With that, he turned and leapt into the lake behind him, causing an unnaturally large splash to erupt from it, which drenched the two bewildered observers.

"Aargh!" Finnian cried. "How could he do that to me? What a wicked sorcerer he is."

"Never mind, Finnian," Brian replied. "You lost your gold, but you've still got me as your friend, and I'll be with you forever."

"Thanks, Brian," he said, brushing water from his eye. "I guess we ought to head back to Dublin. Let's have some more poitin before sundown as well. Perhaps we can catch a rainbow to get there."

The two companions were in luck as it was just starting to rain.

12.

The adventures of Finnian the leprechaun 4

Hugh and Jennifer Ripley were browsing at the boot fair near their home in East Sussex. It was a sunny summer day, and it was hectic. The couple. both in their 70s, hadn't seen much to interest them until an ornate wooden box caught Jennifer's eye amid a pile of bric-a-brac.

"Look at that, Hugh," she said and picked it up.

The seller, a middle-aged ginger-haired woman with thick makeup, mumbled. "Two pounds."

"Okay," she replied, and before her husband could react she had handed over a two-pound coin.

"Thank you," the seller responded.

"Why do you want that?" her husband asked.

"It reminds me of an old music box I had as a child," she said, and she opened the brown wooden object by its hinges. Inside was a small purple bag. She took it out and felt it between her fingers. It had a velvety texture and was empty.

"Nice," she said and placed it back in the box.

They walked around for another half an hour but saw nothing else that they wanted, so Hugh drove them both back home so they could have their Sunday lunch.

Their daughter and grandchildren were due to visit that day with the grandchildren staying overnight. They arrived shortly after three o'clock. After chatting awhile, the children's mother, Louise, left the children with her parents and the boy, Michael, aged nine and his sister Eva, aged eight, spent the day playing in the garden, which was a sizeable one. They had pretended sword fights with wooden sticks and spent a lot of time looking at the goldfish in the garden pond.

Eventually, it got late, and after their grandmother had made them all dinner, they went to bed. The children had a room each as it was a big house. It must have been at around midnight that Eva tiptoed past her sleeping grandparent's room and tapped on the door of her brother. There was no answer, so she opened the door slightly and hissed, "Michael!"

Silence for a while. Then, a slight stirring.

"Michael!" she hissed again.

"What is it?" he answered sleepily.

"I think there's someone downstairs."

"What?"

"Someone is moving about downstairs."

"Probably, grandad."

"No, they're both asleep."

"Have you checked?"

There was silence for a few seconds as Eva looked into the old couple's room.

"They're both in there, Michael. Somebody has got in the house."

"I don't believe it!" Michael almost shouted.

"Ssh," his sister hissed again. "Let's find out who it is."

Then, they both heard the noise of a chair moving from the living room.

"I heard that!" Michael exclaimed. "What if it's burglars?"

"Let's go down quietly and find out."

After a pause and then a groan, he replied, "Okay."

Then, both the children, clad in pyjamas, slowly descended the stairs. They didn't creak, and both children were breathing very slowly so as not to be noticed by their visitors.

Another noise, then a strange muttering voice

"Who the hell is it?" Michael whispered.

Then they reached the base of the staircase and opened the door to the living room from where the sounds were coming. The door opened slowly but easily, and eventually, the two children beheld the sight of the intruder, and neither could believe their eyes.

A man stood with his back to them. An absurdly tiny man of about three feet in height. He was all clad in green clothes, the colour of grass. He had on a green top hat and green shoes. He was holding the wooden box their grandparents had bought at the boot fair in one hand and the small purple bag that was in it in the other.

Eva gasped too loudly for the visitor to span around, dropping the box on the carpet as he did so.

"Who's there?" he called out and saw them immediately. Their eyes were wide and alarmed at the strange little man in front of them.

"Don't hurt us!" cried Eva.

"And don't wake our grandparents," added her brother.

"I'm not here to hurt anyone," the little man replied, his accent strongly Irish. "I'm here to get the magic pouch that was taken from me recently."

"Magic, what?" Michael said.

The little man held up the purple bag that had been in the box. "My bag and all its gold pieces," he said. "Finally, I've got it back."

The children stared in silence.

"Is this a dream?" Eva asked her brother.

"Does it look like a dream?" the visitor answered. He had a thick ginger beard and piercing green eyes. As they watched, he reached into the empty bag and pulled something out, which he threw onto the carpeted floor. It looked like a small gold coin.

"That's one of my gold pieces," he muttered. "Now, to find the rest."

"But that bag is empty!" Michael exclaimed.

"So is your awareness of magic," the little man snorted. He pulled more coins out and threw them on the floor, where they jingled together. "That's another five," he said.

"Where are you getting them from?" asked the perplexed girl. "Are you a magician?"

"No, I'm a leprechaun, and this pouch is connected to the spirit world. That is where I've been storing a lot of my gold coins."

Eva screamed a little.

"Shut up, sis, you'll wake Nan and Grandpa," Michael whispered.

"He says he's a leprechaun, Michael. Like something out of a storybook."

"Yes, and I suppose you'll be wondering if I'll give you any of my gold." the man replied.

"We don't want your gold," said Eva.

"Don't we?" her brother intervened.

"What use is it to us?" she answered.

"Ah, gold has a lot of uses, my child," the leprechaun answered with a wink. He pulled out more gold coins from the bag and threw them jingling down. Maybe ten this time.

"Are you just going to leave them there?" asked the boy. "You're making the place untidy."

"Don't worry, I will pick them up, Michael Baldwin," he said.

"Did I tell you my name was Michael Baldwin?"

"No," he replied. "And I haven't told you my name is Finnian Coghlan."

"Is it then?"

"Of course, it is!" he almost shouted. "Look, I spend most of my time in Ireland, but my magic bag went missing from there some years ago, and today I finally found it brought to this house."

"What a strange person you are," the girl said.

"Strange!" he replied, laughing. "What is strange is that all you humans go through your whole life never being rich and act as if that's an acceptable state of affairs. That's flipping strange to me."

"Good point," Michael said, nodding. "It's horrible not being rich when you see what good things the rich help themselves to."

"You're a clever boy, Michael," said Finnian, touching his nose in appreciation. "Do what I did. Get yourself rich and quick, or you'll have a miserable life."

"I thought leprechauns granted three wishes," Eva said.

"That's right, Eva," he replied. "But I expect all you will wish for is to be rich."

"Not necessarily. We might wish for world peace."

FInnian laughed again. "Well, good luck with that, considering what a brutal bunch of fear-mongering beasts much of the human race is."

"Could we end wars with a wish?" she asked him.

"The same way you could turn the moon into a lump of cheese," he said. "I've little time for you miserable, horrible humans. I belong to the woods and nature. All you ever do is fight and argue. Us leprechauns are peaceful and gentle people who have never fought a war in the thousands of years we've been around, and as well as that. . ."

Then, there was a noise from upstairs.

"Our grandparents are waking up," Eva whispered.

"Eva!" a voice called from upstairs. The voice of grandad Hugh. "Is that you downstairs? What are you doing?"

"Nothing," she called back. "Just getting a glass of water."

"Is Michael down there as well?"

"He's getting one too."

"Okay, but hurry back to bed afterwards," he called. Then, silence for a little while.

The children looked at the little man, who grinned at them.

"What do we do about him?" Eva asked.

"Well, come on then," their grandfather boomed from upstairs

"Oh, I wish he'd go to sleep," Michael hissed.

There was a slight pause, and then a loud thump could be heard above them.

"Your wish was granted," said Finnian, laughing.

"Did you just grant us a wish?" Eva responded.

"Indeed, I did."

"Can we have another one?" Michael asked.

Finnian shrugged. "Depends what mood I'm in."

He then reached into the little bag until his whole arm seemed to disappear into it. He pulled out another handful of gold coins and threw them on the floor.

"That's the last of them," he said. "Now, I ought to pick them up."

He then placed the little bag on a coffee table and began gathering his treasure from the floor. The children watched as he began to stuff them in the pockets of his suit.

"Can we have some of them?" asked the boy.

"Goodness me no!" he replied. "Leprechauns don't give their gold away. You should know that."

"I didn't know there were leprechauns," he answered.

"Well, you do now," replied Finnian on his knees as he picked up the last coin that had rolled next to an armchair.

"I wish you'd let us have ten gold pieces," Michael said.

"Oh, you wish, do you?" said the little man, fixing him with his piercing green eyes. "In that case, here you are."

He then pulled out ten gold coins from his coat pocket and handed them one by one to the boy.

"Wow, I'm rich!" he said in delight, looking at the heap of coins in his cupped hands.

"But you only have one wish left, so don't waste it."

"Can we really wish for anything?" Eva asked, her eyes shining with delight. She picked up a gold coin from her brother and looked at it closely. "This is amazing."

Before he could answer, something odd happened. A loud thunderclap could be heard outside, and a flash of lightning arced outside, visible through the closed curtains.

"A summer storm," Finnian said thoughtfully. "Or maybe a sign that something is going to happen."

Then, the three of them were startled by a movement from the coffee table. The little bag was moving by itself! It seemed to jump in the air, and then Eva screamed as what looked like a small hand reaching out from it.

"What's that?" she cried in alarm.

"Sure, and begorrah, it's Seamus, so it is!" yelled Finnian. "I've got to get out of here."

Without another word, the tiny man dashed into the kitchen. The children heard the cat flap clang noisily.

"What's happening, sis?" asked her brother as he placed his handful of coins in a nearby vase.

The hand wavered in the air until the pouch dropped onto the floor. Both children could hear a faint noise coming from the bag, like a voice snarling and shouting.

"I don't want to find out Mike," she answered. "Let's get away from here." Then, the children ran upstairs. Another loud thunderclap filled the air.

"Where are you, Finnian?" they heard a faint voice yelling from where they had been.

The children looked at each other, panting heavily at the top of the stairs; they barely noticed their grandparent's bedroom door open and their nan coming out of it.

"What's all this noise?" she asked them. "Your grandad is asleep on the floor. That's unlike him."

"Something happened downstairs," Michael gasped. "There's a. . ."

His sister punched his arm.

"There's a what Michael?" said his nan.

"No, it doesn't matter," he replied.

"If there's something happening downstairs, then I want to know."

Before the children could answer, she was slowly walking down the stairs. The children followed nervously. She opened the living room door and looked around as another bolt of lightning flashed outside.

"There's nothing here," she said. "You kids get carried away."

Michael looked at the vase. The coins were gone. The pouch was back on the coffee table next to the box.

"Why did you take this little bag out of its box?" she asked them and replaced it.

"Oh, it doesn't matter. I wish I were back in bed. "Michael sighed. His sister and nan didn't notice as he suddenly whizzed upstairs without his feet even touching the ground and landed on his bed in his room. He groaned at the waste of the wish and fell asleep.

13.

The Duffield family were walking through the hall of mirrors at the travelling funfair. Seven-year-old Lindsey chuckled as she saw her bloated reflection in one. Her parents were not as interested in it as her. Her uncle Steve appeared amused but seemed like he'd rather be somewhere else.

"Look how fat I am!" she exclaimed happily. They were just about to pass out of the hall when Lindsey caught something odd in her reflection that wasn't a mere distortion. A little man dressed in green appeared briefly and gave her a grin.

"What's that mum?" she asked instantly.

"What's what, darling?" her mum Helen replied.

"I saw a little man in the reflection."

"There's nothing there, now, come on, let's go and get some candy floss."

"Okay, Mum," she remained puzzled.

The four family members strolled through the open air towards the candy floss stall. There was quite a queue, and Lindsey realised she needed the toilet.

"Can I go to the toilet now, mum?" she asked.

"Is it an emergency?"

"Yes."

"Okay. I'll go with you. I know where it is. Dad and Uncle Steve can get your candy floss for you while you're gone."

"Okay, thanks, mum."

The two of them walked through the bustling crowd to the public toilets. "Do you want to buy a goldfish?" a young boy asked them, leaping out in front with the fish he'd presumably won earlier in a little bag of water. The boy's mother ushered him away.

"Go on, Lindsey, I'll wait outside, darling." her mum said.

Lindsey walked into the ladies' toilets. A few other girls were in there and as she passed the large mirror in there to the cubicle, she saw a movement in it. Glancing across, she saw the little man in green again. He had a thick beard and a top hat on and looked very old but kind and wise-looking.

"Hello, Lindsey!" he called from within the mirror. She couldn't understand how she could hear his voice or how the man knew her name. She wanted to reply but the other girls in the room, all apparently unaware of what she saw, put her off. Plus, she needed the toilet urgently. After she'd finished, she went to the sink to wash her hands. The toilets were now empty of other people. She was alone in there. As she washed her hands, the little man leapt out of the mirror, or so it seemed, and she stepped back with a scream. He stood on the ground in front of her, but as she screamed, he seemed to leap back into the mirror, which rippled like water for a second. Her mother, alerted by the scream, came running in from outside.

"What's wrong, Lindsey? What happened?" she cried anxiously.

"Mum, a little man just jumped out of the mirror."

"Now, dear, that sort of thing isn't possible. Don't tell lies to your mum."

"I swear it's true."

"Well, let's just forget about it for now. Have you washed your hands?"

Lindsey nodded furiously. "I want to get out of here, Mum."

"Okay. Let's go, darling. Daddy has some candy floss for you."

The two of them found their other family members, and Lindsey guzzled the pink candy floss with delight. They watched the big wheel, the waltzers and the coconut shy, which Lindsey wasn't interested in. She'd wanted to go to the fair with her nine-year-old brother, but he was ill and was being looked after at home by their next-door neighbour. They went to the fair every year, and today was its first day. It lasted for a week.

Eventually, they all decided to go home and got into Uncle Steve's car. Steve lived alone a couple of miles from his brother Mark and his wife Helen and their children Lindsey and Ian. They didn't know him that well and Lindsey didn't really like him. Lindsey sat in the back of the car next to her mum. She was thinking of the strange man she'd seen. Surely, she wasn't going mad. She had a teenage cousin who'd gone mad and was always in and out of hospital. He'd had drug problems, though, which she certainly didn't.

They were nearly home, about five minutes of the journey left, when Lindsey saw something in the rear-view mirror. The little man's face, and he gave her a wink.

"Mum, it's him again!" she wailed. It was getting dark now, and all the headlights were on.

"It's who again?" asked her mum in exasperation.

The face disappeared. She let out a sigh. "Never mind, mum. I've probably watched too many films."

They reached home, and the car pulled up outside. Steve stayed in the driver's seat as the three of them got out. "Nice to see you all," he called out with a toothless grin.

"Thanks, Steve." Helen called out, but Lindsey didn't acknowledge her strange uncle.

They had dinner, watched a bit of TV and went to their bedrooms. Lindsey shared a room with her brother Ian, who looked very unwell that evening and had been bedridden all day. They'd all visited him on returning home, and he said he was feeling better, but the virus he had was keeping him lying low for now.

As Lindsey and Ian lay in their bunk beds in the dark, Lindsey called out to her brother. "Ian, do you ever see things that can't be real?"

"Like what?" he asked weakly.

"Little strange men. Very small men like a. . . ."she was about to say leprechaun but thought her brother would regard her as mad.

"The only strange man I see is Uncle Steve," he replied.

"You don't like him either, then?" she went on.

"Not really. He has such horrible piercing eyes and always that thick black beard."

They were silent for a while. The clock ticked towards midnight, and Lindsey realised she needed a sip of water. "I'm just going to the bathroom," she said, climbing from her top bunk after putting her bedside lamp on.

"Okay," Ian answered weakly.

Lindsey could hear her parents snoring and tiptoed to the bathroom. She had a plastic beaker put aside to clean her teeth and she often had cups of water in the night in it. She reached for the beaker, which was under the mirrored bathroom cabinet. For a second, she feared looking in the mirror in case the little man appeared. She didn't see him in it , just her freckled face surrounded by thick brown hair. She gulped down the water in the beaker and feeling refreshed, she replaced the beaker and turned to leave the room. As she turned, she heard a voice behind her in a familiar Irish lilt.

"Lindsey, I want to talk to you," it hissed. She spun around and saw the man sitting on top of the wash basin, that same little man in green.

This time, she didn't scream. She felt calm and in control. "Look, who are you?" she asked. "How do you keep finding me?"

"I came out of the mirror," he replied matter of factly. She didn't feel scared. She just sighed despite how preposterous it all seemed.

"OK. Whatever. What do you want to talk about?"

"It's about your uncle," he went on and developed a fierce look on his face.

"Uncle Steve?" she responded, and he nodded immediately.

"What about him?"

"He's an evil man and needs to be punished," was the unusual reply.

"Look, who are you? You know my name somehow. What is your name?"

He leapt off the wash basin to the bathroom floor, his tiny shoes clattering on the surface. "I'm Finnian Coghlan, you know," the little man took off his hat and bowed.

"What a strange name that is."

"Do you really think so?" he added. "Stranger to you is that I'm five thousand years old."

Lindsey felt very tired and didn't want to dispute his odd claim. "Look, can I go back to bed? It's late, and I'm exhausted."

"First of all, you need to know about your wicked uncle. He has terrible things on his computer and has committed terrible crimes against children."

Lindsey held her breath. Her eyes widened.

"Really? What sort of crimes?"

"Things I can't talk to you about, but he needs to be held to account, and I want you to help me bring him into the spirit world to face his punishment."

"Spirit world?" she paused. "I've never heard of such a thing."

"It's the realm of the dead and also a realm of purgatory and redemption."

Lindsey didn't understand. "How do I do such a thing?" she asked wearily.

"In the hall of mirrors at the fair, I can trap him."

"Why don't you just call the police?"

At that moment they heard a loud creaking noise as one of her parents was stirring.

"Lindsey," her dad called, "Who are you talking to?"

Lindsey's heart was hammering. "OH, nobody," she called back. "I think I've been sleep talking."

Finnian looked at her. She couldn't understand the strange things he was talking about.

"Look," she whispered. "Talk to me in the morning as I need to go to bed now."

Finnian gave a salute and then did something extraordinary. He leapt onto the wash basin and jumped into the bathroom mirror, which rippled slightly as he disappeared into it. She gasped and reached out to touch the mirror's surface, which was cool and flat like a mirror should be.

The next day, Lindsey went to school while her brother stayed in bed ill. She got a lift there and back from her dad, and on the way back, he repeated what he'd said to her the night before.

"I wasn't talking to anyone!" the girl shouted.

"All right, all right.”

Finnian had said he'd talk to her in the morning but there was no sight of him. While daydreaming at school, she drew a picture of the little man on a piece of paper, which she discarded after class. “Is Ian better?" she asked her dad, eager to change the subject.

"Yes, he should be back at school tomorrow.”

"Dad, what do you know about Uncle Steve?"

"My brother? Well, he lives alone and doesn't go out much. He's a bit younger than me.”

"Does he have a job?"

"Yes, he works in a supermarket. Why all these questions, young lady?"

"Oh, no reason," she replied and gazed out of the window instead. The rush hour traffic was terrible, and she vowed never to drive herself.

They got home, and when her parents were settled in front of the TV, and she'd checked on her brother, who was now sitting up and able to play his beloved computer games, she cautiously crept into the bathroom and looked in the mirror above the wash basin.

"Finnian," she whispered. “Are you there?"

A long pause. Silence except for the computer game noises from her brother's room that she shared with him. After a few minutes, she gave up and returned to her bedroom. She was about to climb onto her top bunk to read a book when she saw something that made her freeze. The leprechaun was sitting on her bed. He sat cross-legged, watching the computer game her brother was playing, and Ian seemed unaware of the little man's presence.

"Finnian!" she gasped.

Seconds later, a voice from the computer screen boomed, 'Game over.'

Ian turned to her in annoyance. "Look what you made me do," he said and coughed a little.

"But. . ." she began, and then Finnian jumped off the bed and scurried out of the room, muttering to himself. Without acknowledging her brother, she followed the little man to the bathroom.

"Did my brother see you?" she asked earnestly.

He turned to her and said, "Doesn't matter if he did. My business does not concern him."

"Look, what is this all about?"

"I want you to go to the fair with your uncle. I need to capture him there in the mirrors."

"But that's a ridiculous idea, and what exactly has he done?"

"I told you it's too awful to tell a childlike yourself. Suffice to say children have been suffering because of people like him."

"Then why don't you do this to all people who do bad things to children?"

"In good time, my child, I assure you we will."

Lindsey looked thoughtful. "We're going to the fair again on its last day on Sunday. I expect we'll go to the hall of mirrors again. It's my favourite bit of the fair."

Finnian grinned happily. She went on, "Are you going to take Uncle Steve into the mirror the way you go into the bathroom mirror?"

"Got it in one, Lindsey."

"But how are you able to do that?"

They were interrupted by a noise. It was the sound of Lindsey's brother walking across the carpet to the bathroom.

"It's my brother!" she gasped.

"Don't worry, little one," Finnian replied.

The bathroom door opened, and Lindsey's pale brother came in. She turned to Finnian who was now standing in the bathtub. Ian looked at Lindsey and then at the little man.

"Can you see him?" Lindsey asked nervously.

"Looks like a leprechaun." Ian replied with disinterest.

"He's my new friend." she went on. "He's called Finnian Coghlan."

"Really. Well, I need the toilet, so can you both leave me alone, please? "

Finnian chuckled.

"Now, both keep me a secret," he said, "I'll be back, don't worry." He leapt out of the bathtub and disappeared into the mirror.

"Is this a dream?" Ian asked his sister.

"He said Uncle Steve has done some really bad things and wants us to take him to the fair and put him in the spirit world."

"What?" Ian asked, incredulous. "That seems impossible."

Lindsey shrugged and went back to her room. When Ian returned, he asked her, "Can the leprechaun get us a pot of gold?"

"He never mentioned it," she replied.

Perhaps he will reward us with it if we do what he is asking."

He said something strange that we should take Uncle Steve to the hall of mirrors at the fair where he will be taken to the spirit world through a mirror."

"What a load of tosh. You don't believe that, do you?"

"I don't understand it either. I'm a bit scared. What will happen to uncle Steve?"

"Why not find out? Sounds exciting," he said and leapt onto his bed. "I'm feeling better now, and I think I can go with you next time. I really want to go to the fair."

The two children went to sleep. Scared but excited. Eventually, Sunday came around, and the siblings were taken to the fair in Uncle Steve's car. This time, their mother didn't go as she had a headache, but their father went, and the children did not want to tell him about the peculiar leprechaun. They sat in the car looking at the back of their uncle's head, wondering what he was thinking and what terrible crimes he had done.

They arrived at the fair and Ian wanted to have a go at the coconut shy. He did quite well and won a large teddy bear, which their father took to the car.

"Can we go to the hall of mirrors, Dad?" Lindsey asked, slightly nervously. Her dad looked at his brother. "Do you want to go there with her?"

Steve gave a slow and slightly creepy smile. "Of course,," he replied.

"I'll go as well," said Ian. He really wanted to see what would happen.

"Okay. You guys all go there then, and I'm going to have a go at the fruit machines. I don't want your children playing on them and losing all your money."

"Okay, Dad," they said, both tingling with nervous excitement. The three of them walked to the hall, paid the entrance fee and looked around.

"Wow, look at this!" Ian cried in delight. "This makes me look really fat."

Steve and Lindsey stood behind him. Lindsey also laughed at the distortion. There were no other people around, and the children looked at each other wondering what would happen. After a few seconds, a strange muttering noise could be heard.

"What was that?" Steve said in surprise. He turned to face the children with his back to the mirrors. As he did so, a pair of tiny hands emerged from the mirror and grabbed Steve around his shoulders.

"Oh my God!" Lindsey wailed.

"What is this?" Steve called as he stumbled to the ground. Both children now felt sad and guilty.

"Damned child abuser," a faint voice mumbled from within the mirror. The hands grabbed him around the ankles and pulled him into the mirror while he floundered on the floor. He disappeared bit by bit, and the children considered trying to pull him back, but in just a few seconds, he had gone. The mirror rippled a bit and then went still. There was silence, and the children were alone. After a few seconds, Lindsey began to cry. "I wish we hadn't done it now." she wept.

"What do we tell, Dad?" Ian asked. They turned to leave and their father appeared in front of them.

"All right, kids," he said. "Want to go on the big wheel? Where's your uncle?"

"Uncle Steve has gone, Dad." Ian said in a flat voice.

"What do you mean gone?"

Ian pointed to the mirrors. "In there."

Their dad looked at his distorted reflection, which the children were not enchanted by now. "Don't talk nonsense," he said. "Where is he?"

"I think he went back to the car," Lindsey cut in before her brother could reply.

"Okay, we'll see him later then. Let's go and have some more fun, kids."

The children rode on the big wheel and the waltzers, and although that was exciting, both were consumed by dark thoughts of what had happened to Steve and what the leprechaun had done to him. Eventually, they finished their rides and went back to the car, but as they approached it, they saw something even more incredible than anything else they'd seen. Uncle Steve was sat in the driver's seat. He was smiling broadly and not in a creepy way.

"Hello, Steve," their father hailed him. "We had a great time, but the kids are ready to go home now."

The children sat in silence at the back of the car as their uncle drove them home. They were doubting that the man driving really was their uncle. They arrived at the house, and their father leapt out of the car, saying he wanted to check on his wife. So, Lindsey and Ian sat in the back with their uncle, unable to know what to say, but then he called out to them from his driver's seat.

"Okay, kids," he said. "I've learned the error of my ways and I shall turn myself in at the police station tomorrow morning. I have a lot of information on people who've committed similar crimes to me, and I want them to pay for their actions."

The children sat in stunned silence. "There's no need to say anything," he went on. "My sins have found me out, and I don't want to hurt any littler people like yourselves."

"Thank You, Uncle Steve. "Lindsey replied nervously. "We will go and see our mum now.". The two children hastily got out of the car and walked to their front door without looking back.

"How on Earth did that happen?" Ian asked his sister, awe-struck.

They finished their evening meal and went to bed. Neither child could sleep. Both had checked the bathroom mirror to see if Finnian would reappear. When he didn't, they went back to their room. After a few hours, their mother came into the room, and she found them both wide awake. They put the light on and stared at her in earnest.

"I've had a phone call from your uncle," she told them. "He said he'd committed terrible crimes against children, and I don't want either of you to ever see him again."

"Okay, Mum," they said in agreement, and eventually, both could sleep but their dreams were plagued by things they couldn't believe to be real.

14.

The Glendalough leprechaun

It was a lunch break in the comprehensive school cloakroom in east London and fourteen-year-old Jon Norris was sitting alone and thinking about the new girl in class who he was madly in love with. In love, possibly, even though he'd never spoken to her and only made eye contact once. He didn't know much about her other than she was called Lucy Knight and was also fourteen. She had auburn hair, always in a ponytail and beautiful brown eyes. He was lost in an adolescent reverie, knowing that other boys rarely came into the cloakroom during lunch breaks. They were all about playing football mostly which Jon didn't understand as they'd never be good enough to be professional. Most of them anyway.

"What are you doing in here?" a voice suddenly cut through the silence. Jon looked up to see someone peeping around the doorway. It was Gary Amos, another teenager in his class who he really hated. A cocky northerner who Jon knew also fancied Lucy.

"Mind your own business," Jon called back, and Gary disappeared from view.

Jon put his head in his hands and groaned. He'd never felt like this about anyone before, and it felt like it would drive him mad. For years, all he'd want to do was ride his bike and play computer games with his friends, but now this. He collapsed onto the bench, his face up, and let out a loud sigh. He would have stayed like that for the entire break if something hadn't distracted him. It was a chirpy voice in an Irish accent off to his right.

"Well, how are you today, young sir?" it said.

Jon frowned and slowly sat up. It was a voice he'd never heard before, and as he looked across to see where it had come from, he almost fell off the bench in surprise.

"Who on Earth are you?" Jon said.

Standing in front of him was a man, but no ordinary man, an unnaturally short man of about three feet in height and all dressed in green clothes. Trousers, jacket, top hat and even his shoes were green.

"Yes, I am on Earth, as are you," he replied. "My name is Finnian Coghlan and I travel the world meeting people to grant wishes and perform miracles."

Jon stared at him in silence and then exclaimed, "You're kidding!"

"No, not kidding," and he ruffled his thick ginger beard. "I think you have a problem right now and I aim to help you with it."

"Know my problem? How do you know I have one?" Jon answered in disbelief.

"You like the new girl in class. Am I right?"

Jon was silent for a while. "Is someone playing tricks on me?" he said. "Are you even a real person?"

"I'm as real as the day is long."

"Yes, I like the girl. Lucy she's called, but I don't know how to get her interested in me. I also worry that if I don't act quickly, someone else will get her."

Finnian sat on the bench and sighed. "Yes, it's a perennial problem for young boys."

"How can you help me?" asked Jon, eyeing the man with suspicion and incredulity.

"I'm a very old man," Finnian went on. I've loved and lost myself too many times for me to count. Being of a human father and fairy mother, I was always destined to be around for a long time, possibly forever. They said my mother was very beautiful, but I don't remember her. My father died thousands of years ago."

"You what?" Jon cut in. "That's not possible!"

"It is possible and please don't interrupt."

"Sorry."

"Never mind. Yes, I'm five thousand years old, and my birth name was different to the one I use now. I've only used my current name for the last two hundred years. Before then my name was so odd that nobody could say it."

"That's incredible." Jon said. "So, you're not really a normal human then."

"Oh, I'm normal for a leprechaun."

"A what?" Jon cried in excitement.

"Yes, I know. I've met many people over the years and watched them grow old in front of me. I've been in love myself. Over two thousand years ago I was travelling the south of France, or Gaul as it was known then and met a lovely lady who took me into her house and treated me like a husband. I was planning a future for us when a cursed Roman soldier took her away from me, and I never saw her again. Good heavens, how much I hated the Romans. I was so delighted when their empire crumbled."

"That's incredible!" Jon repeated. "What a story."

"I know you believe in me, and I know your parents are very good people. Doing lots of work for charity and helping the homeless. That's why I chose to help you in your tricky situation."

"You mean you'll get Lucy to fancy me?" Jon asked excitedly. "That would be perfect."

Suddenly, the school bell rang loudly, and Jon realised it was time to go back to class. "Thanks for the story." Jon said. "Will I see you again?"

Finnian didn't reply and instead mysteriously touched his nose. He grabbed a large coat hanging from a peg and covered himself with it.

"What are you doing?" asked Jon in puzzlement and lifted the coat off the floor. There was nothing underneath it. The little man had gone.

"Wowee!" Jon said, confused, and went to his class. Double history. He really hated it.

After history class Jon was walking along the corridor when he saw Lucy talking to another girl. "Hello Lucy," he said, a tad nervous.

"Hello," she replied.

Jon wanted to say more but couldn't. As he walked further down the corridor, he saw Gary Amos walking towards him—his round face with a mocking smirk on it.

"She'll never go for you," he said. "A girl like that only likes tough guys like me."

Jon walked on without replying but was deeply hurt. Maybe it was true. Gary played in the rugby team for the school while Jon wasn't even muscular enough to play football. He walked home from school in a sulk. He knew he was skinny and spotty with unfashionable hair. That depressed him a bit.

When his parents asked him how his school day went, he simply replied. "Weird." and would not elaborate.

It was a Tuesday and a November so apart from Christmas nothing for him to look forward to. He hoped he'd see little Finnian again and thought of him all night as he lay in bed.

The next morning, at breakfast before school, his mum asked him. "So, when are you going to meet a girlfriend for us to see?"

Jon laughed nervously. "I've just met a new girl in my class. She's very pretty but I don't think she'll be interested in me."

"Why not?" his father cut in, "You're a handsome teenage lad. I had my first girlfriend when I was twelve."

"Please, Dad," Jon said. "There's this other boy who likes her. I think she might go for him instead."

"Nonsense. I'm sure you can sort him out" his dad replied.

Jon remained in a morose silence as his dad drove him to school. As he pulled into to park, Jon saw Lucy standing by the school's main entrance talking on her phone.

"That's her, dad," he said.

"Well, she is pretty," he commented. "Good luck with her anyway."

"I've got double French this morning," Jon groaned. "I need more luck with that."

"It's the language of love," his dad joked. "You can use some on her."

"Yeah whatever," and Jon got out of the car and walked away. He walked past Lucy but she didn't look up at him. He strained to hear her conversation and she seemed to be talking about a dog. He caught fragments of 'take him for a walk' and 'he's only a puppy' and 'get him a ball'. He went to his class after registration, sat in his chair and was bored stupid for an hour.

At lunch break, he went back to the cloakroom, hoping to see little Finnian again. Lucy wasn't in his French class. She was doing religious studies. He didn't really know why he'd chosen French, but all schoolwork bored him now. He was fourteen and couldn't leave for another two years. His parents wanted him to go to university but his heart wasn't in it. He lay back on the bench, stared at the cracked ceiling and sighed in despair.

"Why hello again!" the voice chirped, and Jon sat up in delight. "Finnian!" he called joyfully.

"Yes, it's me. How are you getting on with your lady friend?"

Jon snorted. "I've barely spoken to her. That horrible git Gary had a go at me for trying to talk to her, and now my parents are asking me about girlfriends and I've really had enough."

"What you need is this my boy," the little man said, and Jon saw he was holding a small glass of clear liquid to him.

"What's that?"

"A love potion I concocted myself. Drink this, and she'll fall in love with you."

"Really?" Jon was incredulous. "What's it made of?"

"Don't worry, there's no alcohol in it. It's a mixture of special ingredients you can get from the spirit world. Not alcoholic spirits, I should point out, although I'm partial to them myself."

"You mean I drink that, and she'll instantly love me?"

"Absolutely."

"Wow! She is in my science class this afternoon. I could try and talk to her then."

"A whole different type of Bunsen burner," Finnian chuckled. "Go on. Take a swig."

Finnian held out the glass to Jon, who took it and looked suspiciously at the little man.

"Can I really trust you?" he said.

"You won't know until you try," Finnian sighed.

"OK" Jon said and swallowed the liquid. It tasted slightly of apples, but otherwise nothing else.

"I bid you farewell, Casanova," Finnian said, removing his hat and bowing.

At that moment, the school bell went off to herald the next lesson, and Jon left the little man, holding his empty glass, behind. He really wanted to get to his science class and meet Lucy. The excitement was killing him.

In science class, the teacher, a dull man called Mr Dove, was talking about the biology of flowers and plants, but Jon kept gazing over at Lucy, and whenever he did, Gary would gaze over at him looking suspicious and angry. She did look at him at one point and smiled making Jon's heart nearly skip a beat. The teacher rambled on for ten minutes before telling the class to get into groups of two to do an experiment. Jon looked at Lucy, who looked up at him, and she got out of her chair to walk to his table.

"I want to work with you," she said to him. Jon was sitting with two other boys at his table who would work with each other. Lucy sat down next to Jon and then did something amazing, putting her arm around his neck and kissing him on the side of his face.

"Wowee!" Jon exclaimed. He'd never been kissed like that before.

Mr Dove didn't see this incident, but Gary did. Jon saw him shaking with a jealous rage.

"Sir, they're not allowed to do that!" he cried out.

"Do what?" Mr Dove asked, annoyed. "Pay attention, Amos, this is for your own good."

"I think you're really handsome, Jon," Lucy whispered in a husky voice.

This time, Mr Dove did notice. "What's going on with you two?" he called. "The time for petting is after school. Not now."

Jon blushed with delight. This was everything that he wished would happen and he happily got to work on the class experiment with his crush while Gary would eye them with surprise and annoyance.

After science class, it was the end of school, and Jon asked Lucy if she wanted a lift home. She politely declined saying her mum was getting her. Jon was wondering if Finnian's magic drink was wearing off but then Lucy whispered in his ear, "I can meet you after school Friday if you want. Maybe we can go to the movies."

"Oh, hell yeah!" Jon answered in delight. Overjoyed at this he walked away along the corridor and didn't notice the foot sticking out of a doorway, which tripped him over.

"Hey, watch where you're going," he called as he picked himself up.

"No, you watch where you're going," came the angry reply, and Jon saw his love rival standing in the history classroom doorway. His blotchy face like thunder. He had a blonde crewcut and a thin scar on his right cheek from a rugby injury. "You stay away from my girl," he snarled.

"Your girl!" Jon exclaimed, eyeballing the thug. "You don't even talk to her."

"That's right, you don't," came another voice. The boys looked over and saw Lucy standing in front of them.

"Who do you think you are, Gary?" she said. "You're not God's gift to women. I can like somebody like him if I want to."

Gary flushed an angry red and walked away.

"Sorry about him, Lucy," Jon said. "Do you really like me that much?"

"I'll tell you when we meet up Friday," she said and kissed him briefly on the cheek before walking away in the direction of the retreating Gary.

Puzzled, Jon got his lift home, not knowing what to say to his dad, and all evening, he lay in bed wide awake. At about two in the morning he decided to get some fresh air, and he tiptoed downstairs while his parents and sister were asleep. He went out into the back garden. There was a slight breeze on that chilly November night as he stood in his dressing gown. There was a small oak tree in his back garden and he noticed a movement in its branches and then saw the little man climbing down it. None other than Finnian Coghlan.

"Hello, Finnian!" Jon cried with joy. "Your magic potion worked, and we're going on a date!"

"What did I tell you?" Finnian said, smiling, standing in front of the teenager. "Never underestimate the powers of the little people."

"Do you think she'll marry me one day?"

"Whoa! One thing at a time. I'm five thousand years old and never married, so don't expect things to be that easy."

"How long will the magic potion work for?"

"Oh, it will have worn off by now."

"Really?" Jon was dismayed. "So, she'll lose interest in me?"

"I can't help you with everything. Sometimes, you have to use your own initiative. Faint heart ne'er won fair maid."

"Have I got a faint heart?"

"That's for you to decide."

Jon sat down on a garden chair and put his head in his hands. "I've never felt like this about anyone before," he said with a sigh.

"Oh, I've felt like that many times in all my years, young Jon. On countless occasions I've loved and lost and eventually accepted I'd always remain alone."

"So, you're a lonely old leprechaun?"

"I like my own company sometimes," he said, shrugging

"Well, I don't!" Jon snarled, getting to his feet, "And I don't want that horrible Gary taking her off me."

"Sometimes you have to accept loneliness," said Finnian sadly, shaking his head and looking down at the ground.

"Can't you give me more love potion?".

"That was just to give you a head start. I'm letting you do the legwork from now on. If you want to keep her interested just keep being yourself."

"Oh, what's the point?" Jon groaned, sitting down again, head in hand. "I'm too young for this."

"Yes, and I'm too old for this," Finnian replied.

"So, when I meet her Friday, what should I say?" he looked up curiously.

Finnian held his hands aloft, grinned and said, "Whatever you want to say."

With that, he scampered over to the oak tree, into the branches and vanished from sight.

15.

The Glendalough Leprechaun 2

It was midnight in Stratford-upon-Avon, and a married couple from Chicago were walking along the deserted streets towards the statue of Shakespeare, which stood near his birthplace.

"Just beautiful, Wendy," said Stan to his wife. "This man's amazing words changed the world."

It was July and fairly warm, so both wore just light clothes. Wendy and Stan gazed up at the statue for a few minutes, neither saying anything. There was a full moon, and in the background, the ancient building of Shakespeare's birth was vaguely in view.

"What could I say to him if he were alive," Wendy said dreamily, "What a beautiful soul he must have had."

After a few minutes, they were about to leave and return to their hotel when a movement caught their eyes at the base of the statue. There was a flash of green, and then a tiny man emerged into their sight. He raised a hand and hailed them in an Irish lilt.

"Good evening to you, good people," he said. "I see you are looking at a representation of the greatest writer who ever lived."

"What the. . ." Stan exclaimed. He had never seen a person so small, not even in a magazine.

"Don't look so surprised," the little man went on, "I mean you no harm. I am Finnian Coghlan, the leprechaun, and like you, I am visiting the birthplace of the great bard."

Wendy and Stan could only stand and stare in disbelief in that silent street. The visitor was barely three feet tall and all dressed in green with a green top hat and a ginger beard. His eyes sparkled like diamonds.

"Did you say you were a leprechaun?" Wendy asked. "I never believed in such things."

"But you believe that this great man existed," said the little man, pointing up at the statue. "So why not me?"

"Shakespeare was a real person," said Stan. "The evidence of his existence is in his writing."

"Yet have you not seen drawings of leprechauns?" the man said, grinning broadly.

"I've seen drawings of lots of things. That doesn't mean that they exist," Stan replied.

"How would you feel if I said you could talk to Shakespeare right now, as you are talking to me?" he went on.

"That's impossible!" Wendy scoffed. "He's been dead for centuries."

"Nothing is impossible with the little people," he answered, laughing slightly. "I myself am five thousand years old."

Stan and Wendy stared in silence. They both began to wonder if they were dreaming.

"I think we'd better go, Wendy," Stan said to his wife, a little unsettled. "Let's go back to the hotel before I have a breakdown."

They both turned to leave and began walking nervously away.

"Wait a minute!" called Finnian. "I need to show you something."

Wendy and Stan stopped and looked around, and they saw something which neither could comprehend. The little man was perched on the top of the statue and was seemingly sprinkling a gold-coloured dust over it. He began mumbling some kind of incantation, and the couple's jaws dropped as the statue appeared to move by itself. It raised its hands to its head, which caused a bizarre creaking noise.

"What am I seeing?" cried Stan in disbelief.

The leprechaun leapt off the statue's head and landed like a cat on the floor next to it. The statue itself seemed to shake its head and then took a step off its pedestal.

"Good heavens, what is happening?" Wendy screamed.

"Don't be afraid!" Finnian called. "He just wants to talk to you."

"Talk to me?!" Stan repeated. "It's a statue, and statues don't talk."

"Don't talk!" exclaimed a voice, a loud booming voice that seemed to come from the statue itself. It took a few steps towards the couple, who were backing away in terror.

"What's happening, Stan?" yelled his wife.

"Much ado about nothing!" the leprechaun yelled with a laugh. "Perhaps you're having a midsummer night's dream."

As the statue moved forward, it made a metallic squeal, and then it raised its left hand and rubbed its bald head.

"Don't you wish to talk to the great man?" Finnian cried, still laughing hysterically.

The statue stopped and looked around at the laughing little man. Finnian immediately stopped laughing and gave a comical salute to the statue.

"Pardon me, your greatness," he said to it seriously. "I was just granting the wish of two people who wished to talk to Shakespeare."

"We didn't wish for that," Wendy answered, shaking slightly.

Her husband put his arm around her shoulder. "Calm down, Wendy," he said.

The statue turned to face the terrified couple. It seemed to be smiling, but the light wasn't great.

"How wonderful to meet fans of mine," a voice boomed. "People who appreciate what a genius I was."

"Oh yes," Stan mumbled nervously. "Certainly, a genius. All my life, I've tried to write poetry, but I can't compare to you,"

"Few people can," it said distantly, its voice having the Midlands accent of the region. "I expect you want to know if I experienced a dream after my death, as in my Hamlet speech."

"W-we don't want to bother you over things like that. "Wendy stammered. "We just like to appreciate your genius as it is."

"That's good," it said and fell silent. The couple saw Finnian standing nearby, and further down the street an old man was walking along who did not acknowledge the peculiar scene that was going on. Either he couldn't see them, or this was some kind of shared hallucination.

"I expect you are wondering if death is a lonely experience," the statue said. The couple noticed the lips of the statue didn't move as it appeared to speak. "So many millions have asked the same question, but I can't tell you the secret. As Hamlet said, 'no wanderer returns.'"

"But you're talking to us now," Stan cut in.

"All because of a leprechaun enchantment," it replied. "Do you believe in such things?"

"We don't know what to believe," said Wendy. "We came to this world-famous town because of Shakespeare, and I've seen every play acted out somewhere or other over the years and read every poem."

The statue appeared to shrug. Then the little leprechaun began walking over to them.

"How did you make this happen?" Stan asked, his mouth dry. "You're a genius yourself."

"I am most flattered," said the little man and he took off his hat and bowed to them. He stood up straight and looked up at the statue. "But all's well that ends well."

Then he clicked his fingers, and both Stan and Wendy recoiled from a blast of white light. When the light disappeared, they saw the Shakespeare statue back on its pedestal and the little man in green had gone.

Stan rubbed his eyes.

"Was that a dream?" he asked in bewilderment to his wife.

"I dreamt it as well, Stan," she replied, laughing nervously.

They both walked up to the statue, bracing themselves for another movement from it. The slight summer breeze ruffled their hair, but nothing else happened.

"I think I need to go back to bed," Stan groaned.

"To sleep perchance to dream," his wife added, and they both turned and walked away.

16.

Tim Griffin had fallen asleep in his dinghy. After filling it with air and pushing it out from Brighton beach on a spring day when the beach had mostly been deserted despite the fine weather, he was now adrift. He'd been asleep for over an hour with the boat's single oar laying across him. Nobody had seen him go and as he started to slowly awaken, he realised that the Sussex coastline was now a speck in the distance.

Tim gasped and sat up quickly. He looked around himself and realised he was stranded in the English Channel. Apart from another large vessel quite a long way away, he could see nothing but sea.

"OH my God!" he yelled. Then, as he gaped in horror at where the coastline should be, he saw a movement ahead of him. Something that looked green and at first he thought it was a fish leaping out of the water, but as it got closer he realised, half with relief, that what he saw was a little man in a green suit running on the surface of the water towards him. He was relieved because no matter how alert he seemed, this had to be a dream. Such things did not happen in the real world. He put a hand in the sea water, which was ice cold, and splashed his face with it. He shook his head to clear it and then looked around again.

Now, the little man was just ten feet away. He had stopped running and stood on the surface of the water regarding thirty-five-year-old father of two Tim with a stern stare with his hands aggressively on his hips.

"Who are you? Weirdo in my dream." Tim said to him.

"Me a weirdo?" the little man replied in a thick Irish accent. "Surely not as weird as a man who falls asleep in a dinghy without a mobile phone and gets pulled out to sea."

He took a couple of steps nearer, and instinctively, Tim grabbed the boat's oar and held it in a threatening way. "Only Jesus can walk on water. "Tim responded.

"Well, so can the little people," he replied. "My name is Finnian Coghlan and..."

"I don't care what your name is. You're in my dream, and I want to wake up."

"Really?" Finnian exclaimed with a grin. "Let me help you with that." at which point Finnian bent down and began splashing water onto the dinghy and into Tim's face, who cursed and spluttered under the attack.

"OK, lay off!" he shouted.

Finnian stopped and folded his arms, regarding the man with piercing green eyes. "You're not a good man, Tim Griffin. I'm here to punish you." he intoned.

"How do you know my name?" he began and then tailed off laughing. "This is one crazy dream."

"So if you're dreaming." snarled Finnian. "Why don't you walk on the water like me, or maybe you can swim for the beach as you clearly can't drown?"

Tim sat in silence, the sea nudging his dinghy. Faint calls of gulls could be heard in the distance. The breeze was gentle and blew Tim's wispy blonde hair and Finnian's ginger beard. He also wore a green hat and green clothes, but it was his green shoes balancing on the surface of the water that made his appearance seem absurd.

"What do you want from me?" Tim asked. "I need to row back to shore."

"I'm here to talk to you about a schoolboy you once knew. A young Irish lad called Chris Kelly."

"Sissy Chris." Tim retorted, almost laughing. "I hated him. So did my mates, "

"Of course you did," Finnian answered coldly. "That's why you bullied him mercilessly.

"He played with dolls when he was thirteen. He was a right queer."

"So, you won't be too upset to know that he committed suicide last week."

Tim shrugged. "I don't care. We all have to die."

"You spiteful low life," Finnian growled and reached for the dinghy with his tiny hands rocking it viciously. Tim almost fell out and swore at the leprechaun.

"Stop that," Tim shouted, and Finnian stopped and stepped back.

"I hate bullies." he went on at the stranded young man. "They need to know the error of their ways."

At that point Tim aimed a punch at the little man but missed and plunged into the icy cold channel. Luckily for him he was a strong swimmer and was able to clamber, gasping, onto his feeble little boat.

"Young Chris wrote a suicide note, don't you know." Finnian went on. "He blamed school bullies for ending his life. In particular, you, Mr Griffin."

"Just get stuffed, you freak. It's none of your business. Sissy kids deserve to be bullied. I don't care that he's dead."

"You're a glutton for punishment." the man on the water laughed, and he grabbed the boat's oar, wrenching it from Tim's grasp.

"Give that back!" the bully shouted.

"Or what?" Finnian yelled back, and he hurled the oar away, where it sank out of sight in the depths of the channel.

"OK, I was a bully. I'm sorry. Now, will you leave me alone?"

"Leave you alone?" the leprechaun said quietly. "How do you return to the shore now?"

"I'll get the attention of a nearby boat."

"How will you do that? You don't have a distress flare."

Tim slumped back in his boat, closed his eyes and mumbled to himself.

"You're a spiteful and wretched man, Timothy Griffin. "Finnian went on. "I wish all such bullies got the treatment I'm giving you."

"Go and find them then, and leave me alone."

"You'll never get to land without me. You're literally up the creek without a paddle."

"I'm hungry," Tim said. "I need to get back to the beach, or I'll starve out here."

At that moment, Finnian looked down at his feet. He got into a crouching position and then quickly lunged towards the sea and grabbed something from the water with both hands. He stood up with the wriggling object that Tim could see was a mackerel.

"Fancy a fish to eat, Tim?" he shouted and hurled it at the man's face. It splattered onto his dinghy, and Tim recoiled and knocked the fish back into the water. "You crazy little…" he exclaimed.

"Not too partial to fish myself either, Tim," Finnian said. "I'd rather have an apple."

"I don't care about you, you crazy whatever you are."

"You don't care about anyone but yourself," Finnian snapped.

"I've got a wife and kids!" Tim shouted back. "They need me."

"Young Chris Kelly was shy around girls. He was no queer, as you called him. He never had a girlfriend and hanged himself alone in his bedsit. His mother died when he was twelve, and you bullied him over that as well."

"How do you know all this? Are you the judgement of God or something?"

"No, but I wish I was."

"It's not my fault about that poor specimen, sissy Chris. Nobody liked him anyway and..."

Finnian had heard enough. He grabbed at the front of the dinghy and then began tearing at it with his teeth.

"What are you doing?" Tim screamed. "You'll sink my boat."

"Sink sink!" Finnian shouted as the boat began to deflate. "Like the Titanic where better people than you were killed."

As the boat lost its air, the icy cold water of the channel pumped into it and Tim slid in feet first. "Please, mister." he cried. "Please help me!"

Tim was a strong swimmer but he knew he'd be no match for the strong currents of the channel, and still wearing his clothes, which would weigh him down even more. He flipped over onto his back as the dinghy slid out of sight. He was gasping for air in the freezing water, and although he maintained his floating position, he could feel himself losing consciousness. Finnian stood on the water in front of him. His face showed no emotion, and then, for Tim, everything went black.

Darkness. Silence. Then, the sound of seagulls, and he sat up with a start. He looked around and gasped in disbelief. He was back in his boat! His oar was lying across him, and Brighton Beach was now barely thirty metres away. Plus, his clothes were bone dry. So it was all a dream, he concluded and slumped back in his dinghy. He lay there, eyes closed for several minutes, and then he sat up and paddled slowly to shore. As he did so, he noticed something in the dinghy with him. It was a small green envelope he'd never seen before. His hands were shaking a little as he picked it up and tore it open. Inside was a short message on a white card in capital letters. I WILL BE WATCHING YOU.

Tim laughed and tore it up. "You don't scare me." he snarled and hurled the torn pieces into the sea. As he did so, he heard a rumbling noise from under the boat, which made him freeze. Out of nowhere, a large wave struck the dinghy and knocked him overboard, with the boat capsizing. Wheezing in shock, Tim turned his boat back upright and clambered back onto it. He immediately began rowing furiously. Now, people on the beach were shouting and pointing in his direction. The currents were strong, but adrenalin made him able to deal with them and soon he was clambering on the beach, retching and spluttering.

"What the hell happened to you?" an old man asked. "I've never seen a wave that big before."

Tim didn't reply. He was gasping for breath after the strange ordeal. He tried to tell himself it was a dream but then he recalled the message left in his dinghy, which had seemed very real. He'd often taken his dinghy out from the beach but would never do it again. The strange little Irish man, whoever he was, had taught him a powerful lesson, and he vowed to make himself a better person. As he lay face down on the pebbles, he did something he'd not done since childhood. He began crying.

17.

In a tree house in Hastings, two young sisters were eating apples. Amy, who was seven, and Sarah, who was nine, were enjoying a hot sunny day in their back garden. They had wealthy parents who liked to indulge their three children, including their bad-tempered fifteen-year-old brother. What Amy and Sarah didn't know was that this particular day in late July would be a day they would never forget. Sarah finished her apple and hurled the core into the garden. As Amy took her last bite of her one they were both startled by a voice that came from a higher level of the tree house. The level where a small sleeping hut had been built by their father

"Aha, Seamus, you'll never find me here," it said.

Sarah gasped and stared at Amy. The voice was musical and Irish and was a voice they'd never heard before.

"Who was that?" whispered Amy nervously.

"Let's find out," replied Sarah, and they slowly climbed the small rope ladder within the wooden platforms. The sister's mother wasn't happy about the tree house, thinking the children would fall out and be badly hurt, but their father knew they were a clever couple of kids who would not let that happen, and after a year of the house being in the tree he'd been right. Not a single accident, but he'd not reckoned on strange people appearing in the house, which Amy and Sarah were now beginning to investigate.

"My gold is safe here, Seamus O'Grady. I have found the perfect hiding place." The voice was just feet away from Sarah as she climbed. She nervously looked inside the large wooden sleeping room that her father had cleverly made and could not believe what she saw.

A little man, who may have been three-foot-tall, was laying on the pile of cushions the girls had put there. He was all dressed in green with a green hat and a thick ginger beard. He was caressing a black pot that appeared to be full of gold-coloured coins. His eyes drifted around, and he saw her looking at him.

"Saints alive!" he yelled. "Stay away, Seamus, this is my gold."

He leapt in the air, banging his head on the wooden beams above him, which made his hat fall off, exposing a pink bald head. He grabbed the hat and shrank back in fear.

"My name is not Seamus," Sarah told him, both alarmed and amused. "I'm Sarah, and this is the tree house my father built. So how did you get here?"

Before the man could answer, Sarah's sister pulled alongside her, making the peculiar man recoil again, and he tentatively reached for his black pot of coins.

"This is my treasure, and my name is Finnian Coghlan, young girl. I mean, you no harm, but my rival is after me, and I need somewhere to hide."

"How long have you been hiding here?" Amy asked, not at all afraid. "My name is Amy."

"You may ask how long I've been in Hastings, " he said. "I watched the battle here when I was a younger man."

"What battle?" Sarah asked.

"You know! The one where the king got an arrow in his eye."

"The Battle of Hastings!" Amy and Sarah cried in unison. "That was a thousand years ago!" Sarah added." How old are you?"

"About five thousand," Finnian replied nonchalantly. "Give or take a few decades. To be honest, I've lost count."

"That's impossible," said Amy. "Nobody can live that long."

"Aha, you see," said Finnian, smiling. "Us leprechauns can do miracles."

"A leprechaun," said Sarah, puzzled. "They don't exist. Like fairies."

"Don't exist!" Finnian laughed. "Then who am I then?"

"Wow," said Amy. "This is incredible."

The girls looked at each other while Finnian rubbed his head and replaced his hat.

"Please can I stay here," he said. "If Seamus finds me, he'll steal my gold. If you are good to me, you can have some of my gold."

"What do we need with gold?" Sarah asked scornfully. "Our parents are rich."

"Really?" Finnian replied, looking thoughtful.

"No, not really rich," Amy quickly added. "Really, Sarah! We're not millionaires, but we go to a good school and have wonderful holidays all around the world."

Finnian was silent, then changing the subject he picked up a book that had been under the cushions.

"That's my book," Amy said to him. Finnian held it up and looked at the front cover. "The magic faraway tree" he read.

"It's my favourite book. Please put it down," said Amy.

Finnian laughed and threw it in the air. A flash of light came from it, and it landed back in the little man's hand, now as an oblong of what looked like gold.

Amy gasped, "What have you done?" and edged back nervously.

"This is worth more than a book, "Finnian answered and placed the lump on his pot of coins. He then reached into a corner and pulled out an apple, which he bit into.

"And who said you could eat our apples? "Sarah asked, crossly folding her arms.

"I get hungry sometimes, as I'm sure you do, " he said.

"Well, we.." Sarah began, but then a man's loud voice cut her off.

"Amy! Sarah! Dinner is ready. Chop chop!"

"I told you so," Finnian grinned, taking another bite.

Amy looked at Sarah with doubt in her eyes. "Can we leave him here like this?" she said.

"Never mind, I'm starving. "Sarah replied and began to descend the ladder. Finnian gave Amy a wink, and she followed her sister.

"Bye-bye, girls, and if you see Seamus, don't tell him I'm here, please."

"Oh, bother him," Sarah said as the girls reached the ground. They would not tell their father, but what would become of Finnian?

Amy and Sarah ate their dinner quietly with their older brother, Sam and their parents, Simon and Sharon.

"It's really hot today, isn't it, guys?" their father asked. He was a tall man, muscular and dark-skinned. He worked on building sites around the south east and had a lot of money.

"Climate change has made it that for years," their mother answered gloomily. She was a short blonde woman who worked as a secretary.

"You're so pessimistic, Sharon, " their father replied.

"Can we go back to the tree house after dinner, Dad?" Amy asked enthusiastically. "It's not too late."

"Yeah, sure," he said without looking up. "Back in bed by eight o'clock, though, please, and no sleeping in the tree again."

Amy looked excitedly at Sarah, who also looked delighted.

"Tree houses are boring, " said their brother Sam. "I'd rather play football."

"And get covered in mud again, Sam. Not today, you don't." replied their mother.

Sam muttered an unintelligible reply.

***

After dinner, the girls rushed into the garden and began to climb the tree. It was a very strong oak tree, surely over a hundred years old. They couldn't wait to see their peculiar new friend. Sure enough, they saw him lying on the cushions, fast asleep and snoring loudly. He'd placed some of his gold coins on his green suit in which he looked very hot. Beads of sweat were visible on his brow.

"Finnian, wake up, " Sarah called and shook the little man.

"Seamus, no, it's mine. You can't have it, " yelled Finnian as he woke with a start. The gold coins dropped off him as he sat up and clinked onto the wooden floor. One of them rolled lazily across the planks and dropped out of the tree onto the garden below.

"It's not Seamus. It's us, " answered Amy.

"You're making me lose my gold, "he replied grumpily, gathering in the fallen coins and placing them back in his pot. "Be careful, will you."

"Gosh, it's hot," Sarah said, flopping onto a cushion.

"Because of climate change," said Amy.

"Huh?" Finnian said scornfully. "This isn't hot, and us little people can make sure climate change won't be a problem."

"Really?" answered Sarah. "How?"

"I've been doing miracles all around the world for five thousand years, and I can do anything, "he replied confidently.

Amy and Sarah glanced at each other. "What do you want from us, Finnian?" asked Amy.

"Just please let me stay here for a few days so Seamus can't find me. If you see him, you'll remember him. He has a red suit and a very long grey beard and smokes a pipe."

"And he is three feet tall like you, I suppose?" said Sarah.

"Of course," answered the leprechaun. "But he's not as nice as me."

"What sort of powers do you have?" Amy asked with excitement in her voice.

"Oh, anything," he said, with a dismissive wave of his hand. "I can turn things into gold and can make myself invisible to adults and..." he stopped and looked up. "But why should I tell you? I don't know how much I can trust you."

"So you can't read minds!" Sarah laughed. Finnian sat up, rubbing his beard. "Look, I'm not there to bother you," he told them. "I'm just hiding from my sworn enemy who wants to steal my gold and humiliate me." He picked up the block of gold that was once Amy's book and looked at it thoughtfully.

"Look, if you help me, I will reward you handsomely. I can make you rich beyond your wildest dreams."

"We don't want your money, Finnian, but we will help you. Won't we, Amy?" her sister nodded enthusiastically.

The little man flopped back onto the cushions, dropped the lump of gold and gave a huge sigh.

"Thank you so much," he replied. "You seem like good children. I think I can trust you, but I must warn you that you must not show any of my gold to your family. Otherwise, a terrible curse will befall you, which has happened to children I met before who betrayed me."

"Oh, of course," Amy said, slightly nervously. "What sort of curse?"

"Don't betray me, and you won't find out."

"We won't, Finnian, and we won't let Seamus know you're here, "said Sarah. "Look, it's getting late, and we have to go back to our house now. You can stay here overnight, and there are more apples if you want them. We won't tell anyone about you or your gold."

"I'm obliged to you. Off you go, little ones and I'll see you tomorrow," he said, contently picking up another apple.

The two children descended the tree, both beside themselves with excitement. Both were too buoyant to sleep and were really looking forward to the next day of this adventure.

The next day was also hot and sunny, and a Sunday with the school holidays stretching out in front of them. Amy and Sarah excitedly bolted down their breakfasts and then ran to the back garden when Sarah saw something that made her jump and hold out a warning hand to her sister. Amy looked as well and saw their brother Sam under the tree, looking at something he'd picked up from the ground.

"It's one of Finnian's coins," Sarah told her nervously. "We mustn't tell him the truth."

Sam held the coin in the palm of his right hand and walked slowly towards the back door where his sister's stood anxiously. He glanced up at them and asked. "Is this one of your things?"

Nervously, Amy replied, "What is it?"

"Looks like an old coin, but I've never seen one like this before. I'll show dad."

"You don't have to do that, " Sarah babbled in concern. He stared at her bemusedly, "Why not?"

"Oh, Dad isn't interested in old coins."

"How do you know? Have you asked him?" he then walked past them into the house out of sight.

"We can't tell them the truth, or there will be a curse on us, "said Amy.

"Let's ask Finnian, " said Sarah, and they climbed the tree cautiously up the strong rope ladder put in by their talented father. Once again, they saw Finnian asleep on the pile of cushions, his arms cradling his pot of gold. As they approached, he opened one eye and then slowly sat up.

"Hello again," he said chirpily. "Isn't it a lovely morning?"

"Yes, it is," replied Sarah. "But we are a bit worried about our brother."

"Why, what has he done?" Finnian asked, his eyes wide.

"He found one of your gold coins and took it away."

Finnian laughed. "Ha. It'll be no use to him. Gold taken away from a leprechaun by a human without his blessing becomes worthless iron. As soon as he tries to sell it, the metal ceases to be gold."

Amy and Sarah sat in silence. They noticed a lot of apple cores littered among the cushions. It looked as though Finnian had eaten all of them.

He went on. "Now, don't worry about him. I've plenty of gold left and I might give some to you when Seamus has stopped looking for me."

"So, how will you know when it's safe enough for you to leave?" Sarah asked in exasperation.

"Aha, I'll know when he's gone. Don't worry."

"When he is gone, where will you go?" asked Amy.

"Back to Glendalough, my birthplace in Ireland. I travel by rainbow, but in this hot sun, I can't find a rainbow to help me leave. Seamus knows about my pot of gold because somebody I befriended betrayed me and told him of it. A child like you two. As I told you, bad luck did befall him, and... no, I'd better not tell you about that. I don't want to scare you as you've been good to me." He got to his feet, rubbed his brow slowly and paced up and down, his hat almost brushing the boards above him.

"Seamus is very selfish," he said. "One of the bad leprechauns who only cares about making himself rich and powerful. He cares not for children or his fellow leprechauns. He wants to scare people and use his powers to bad effect. I need to escape from here so he can lose track of me."

"How can we help you escape?" replied Sarah.

"I want you to set a trap for Seamus. I can imprison his soul using my gold as bait, and then he'll be banished for seven years. Then I can be far away where he'll never find me."

He picked up the lump of gold that was once Amy's book and held it up to them. "I can use this and my pot to capture him. Now, will you help me?"

Amy and Sarah looked at each other, their eyes wide, and slowly nodded.

"Yippee!" yelled Finnian, and threw a coin in the air with joy. He then picked up his round pot and poured the coins out onto what was in the corner of the tiny tree house room. They glistened in the light. Finnian took the empty pot and held it up, saying.

"We'll catch him in this, my girls. Ho Ho, it will be such fun."

***

The next day the girls were back in the tree house and listening excitedly as to how Finnian would imprison Seamus to end the bad man's search for gold that wasn't his. The plan was to dangle the gold bar from a tree branch, and then when Seamus walked up to it to, drop the upturned pot on his head to banish him to the spirit world.

"But how will we get him to the tree?" Amy asked, and Finnian produced what looked like a silver whistle from his breast pocket.

"If you blow this whistle, Seamus will follow the sound and come to the tree, "he told them. "You must do it in the evening, so try to get out of the house without disturbing your parents. Find something to tie the gold to a branch and blow the whistle gently. It doesn't have to be too loud, so nobody needs to be disturbed from sleep. You don't have a dog, do you?"

"No, we have a cat," Amy said.

"That's fine. Not a problem, then. Now, we'll try it this evening at about eleven o'clock, and please be careful and don't let Seamus escape, or he'll wreak terrible revenge on us."

The girls' hearts beat excitedly. They were scared, but they wanted to help their friend.

Later Sarah found an old shoelace in a drawer and tied it to the gold bar that had been Amy's book. She climbed the ladder halfway and was able to tie the lace to a lower branch. This took several attempts, but finally, she succeeded, and when she looked up at Finnian, he gave her the thumbs up.

"Well done, my girl," he hissed. It was early evening, and the sky was darkening. The girls realised they'd need a torch to see what they were doing when they tried to capture this mysterious unknown leprechaun.

"OK, girls, go back in the house and come back when your parents and brother have gone to bed," he instructed. Sarah gave him a salute, and the children did as they were told.

Finnian waited impatiently in the tree for hours. It got to midnight, and he began to hiss and curse under his breath. He was about to climb out of the tree when the back door of the house opened, and Amy and Sarah, both in pyjamas, crept quietly out of their house.

"Quickly!" Finnian hissed in annoyance. "Why are you so late?"

"Sam wouldn't go to bed. He was playing computer games until half past eleven, " Amy answered apologetically.

"OK, never mind. We can carry out our plan now."

Finnian clambered down the ladder and stood in front of the girls. They realised how incredibly short he was. Less than three feet tall, he stood, but the passion in his face made him more mature than any child.

"OK, this is the plan," he said and pulled out his silver whistle. He handed it to Sarah, who was shaking a little. "On my instruction," he went on. "Blow this whistle under the tree, and eventually, Seamus will hear it. He'll come over to investigate, see the gold and then we'll get him."

The girls glanced at each other nervously. The moon was full, so there was enough light. They hadn't been able to find a torch. The street lights added further illumination.

"I shall be in the tree with Amy, and I shall drop the pot on his head, which should engulf him entirely and cast him into the spirit world for seven years."

Amy bit her nails nervously. "Are you sure this will work, Finnian?" she said, concerned.

"Of course, it will work!" he almost yelled back. "I've dealt with characters like him before. You don't look this good for five thousand years when you don't know how to look after yourself."

Sarah laughed slightly, and Amy could see the terror on her face.

"But we're only children..." she began, but Finnian waved his hand dismissively. "Don't worry, you're clever enough to help me," he said.

"Now, let's get going. Amy climbs up the ladder with me while Sarah stands by the gold with the whistle."

Amy shot her sister a worried look and ascended the tree after the scampering Finnian, who didn't even need the ladder.

"OK," Finnian whispered down to Sarah. "When I count to three, I want you to blow the whistle and then join us up here. Ready? 1..... 2... 3!"

Sarah blew the whistle. It made a peculiar noise she wasn't expecting. Almost like a cat whining.

"OK, that will summon him. Now get up here quick."

Sarah quickly joined her companions, her heart beating fast, and the three of them looked around the garden for their elusive quarry. For a couple of minutes, they saw nothing, and then Amy noticed a movement in the corner of the garden. At first she thought it was their cat Felix until she saw the flash of red that was the suit of Seamus O'Grady.

"It's Seamus!" Finnian whispered ecstatically, and the girls detected fear in his voice.

The little man appeared out of the shadows. He was as Finnian had described to them. All clad in red with a long beard below his waist and very cruel eyes that darted furtively around. He walked slowly towards the tree, his eyes suddenly fixed on the dangling gold bar. A look of hungry greed crossed his face that alarmed the girls but they remained silent, their hearts hammering.

"I've found you, Finnian Coghlan, "he hissed to himself. "I know you're about somewhere."

Finnian slowly edged towards the end of the protruding platform of the tree house, desperate not to be seen. He held the pot ready.

Seamus was now directly underneath them, and he tried to reach for the hanging bar of gold, but it was too high for him. As he scratched his head, Finnian dropped the pot on him.

Seamus was too slow to react. The pot went over his head and continued downwards, engulfing his entire body. The two girls saw his brown shoes briefly underneath, and then they were gone. The three of them heard his mournful, echoing wail as he was banished into the spirit world.

"Got him!" yelled Finnian in delight and punched the air with joy. "At last!"

The three of them descended the tree and looked more closely at the pot; it had fallen on its side, and a tendril of white smoke drifted from it.

"Oh, thank you, girls" "Thank you, "he hollered, grabbing their hands with joy. "I will never forget this... I..."

"What's going on out here?" a voice shouted from the house. The girls gasped. It was their brother Sam. He was standing in the back doorway in a dressing gown. Finnian immediately scampered up the tree without a sound, leaving the two girls to face their brother, mouthing silently and unable to talk.

"What are you doing?" he went on and walked towards them over the grass.

"And what's that?" he added, pointing to the upturned pot.

"That's our... er..." Sarah began and looked nervously at Amy.

Sam looked more closely at the pot and reached down to touch it, and as he did so, they all heard Finnian clap his hands furiously from up the tree.

"What's that noise?" Sam asked, gazing up into the tree.

They didn't need to answer him, for at that moment, the heavens opened, and torrential rain began to lash down. Finnian could still be heard clapping and the girls suspected he had caused the rain as the three siblings ran into the house.

"You'll be in trouble going out late like that, "their brother went on from inside the house.

"You won't tell mum and dad, will you?" Amy pleaded.

Sam didn't answer and sloped off back to bed. The girls sheepishly went back to their own room and knew they wouldn't sleep while they waited for the morning.

Once again, the next day was hot and sunny. The family had their breakfast, and Sam hadn't told his parents what his two sisters had been up to last night, to their relief. Eventually, Sam went out to play football, and the two girls anxiously returned to the tree that had yielded such an adventure recently. The fallen pot had gone, as had the hanging bar of gold that had once been Amy's book, although the old shoelace remained. The girls glanced at each other and then climbed the ladder. Finnian was not lying on the cushions and the gold coins had gone. They realised their unusual friend had left them. Sarah noticed a small green box in the corner, balanced on one of the cushions. She opened it up, and they saw six gold coins in there. Presumably three each for the girls and a small white card with one word on it, handwritten. 'Thank you!"

The girls looked at each other and shrugged. Their friend was gone, but he'd left them some gold as promised, and they wondered if they'd ever see him again.

18.

Arnold Hudson opened the boot of his taxi and could not believe what he was seeing. Earlier, he'd placed his lunchbox in there and was about to retrieve it when he saw that curled up next to it was a small green-suited man with a ginger beard and green top hat. As the boot opened, the little man sat up and grabbed Arnold by the lapels.

"Don't give me away!" he pleaded in an Irish accent. "Seamus O'Grady is after me. I only got in your car to hide."

Arnold pushed the little man away and stepped back. "Who the hell are you?" he asked. "Are you from a freak show or something?"

"Now that's not nice to call one of the little people a freak, now is it?" the man replied indignantly.

"What are you doing in my cab?" Arnold went on. "I told you. A wicked, evil leprechaun is after me. He escaped from the spirit world and has frightening powers."

"Spirit world?" Arnold asked. "The only spirit I'm interested in comes in a bottle."

"He wants to turn me into a frog, and I know he has the power to do it."

"Just a typical day in New York," Arnold said, scratching his head.

"I've been all over the world. Last week, I was in South Africa, and Seamus nearly found me. I travelled by rainbow to get away and arrived in New York yesterday."

"Yeah, whatever," Arnold answered, picking up his lunch box. "Just clear off now. I'm having my lunch, and then I've got work to do."

The leprechaun froze suddenly and leapt out of the car boot, landing with great agility by the side of the road. "I can hear him" he gasped.

"Hear who?"

Then, a voice cut through to them from further down the street. "I know you're here, Finnian Coghlan!"

"It's Seamus!" Finnian gasped and ran away down a side alley, disturbing litter and an alley cat as he went.

"OK, fat chops, where is he?" came the voice again, closer to Arnold now.

Arnold closed the boot of his cab and looked in more incredulity at what he was seeing. A red-suited man, as short as the other one with an even longer beard, stood in front of him. His green eyes pierced the cabbie. "Who are you calling fat?" Arnold replied.

Without answering, the red-suited man raised his right hand and pointed at Arnold in a threatening way. "Tell me where he went," he hissed.

"I don't know. He just ran off. None of my business." Arnold gestured towards the alleyway that Finnian had run down. "Now, none of you weirdoes disturbing me any more, please." With that, Arnold walked to the driver's seat and sat down to eat his lunch.

The little man walked over to Arnold and said to him, "I have the power to turn you into a frog, so don't mess with me."

"Sure, and I'm John F Kennedy" he replied and waved his hand dismissively at him.

With that, there was a flash of light, and Arnold no longer sat in his cab. A frog was on the seat instead. "Let that be a lesson to you," Seamus sneered at the frog, and he walked towards the alley Finnian had run down. A few steps in, he saw a homeless man huddled against a small fire. He was old and bearded like him.

"You hobo," Seamus said. "Have you seen a man in green go down this alley?"

Without answering, the old man answered. "Can you spare some change, fella?"

"I'm not interested in worthless scum like you," Seamus replied. "Just tell me where he went."

The man didn't reply and held out his hands to the fire in morose silence. Seamus cursed and walked down the alley by himself. After a few minutes, shuddering under a blanket next to the hobo, Finnian crawled out and said to the man.

"Thanks for not giving me away. What is your name?"

"Brandon," he replied.

"OK, Brandon, for helping me, I'll give you three gold coins, and he placed them in Brandon's shaking hands.

"God bless you, man," the homeless man said. "Now you can stay in a hotel and... oh no, I'd better get out of here before Seamus returns. Thanks anyway" So Finnian ran back out of the alleyway to Arnold Hudson's parked cab. He saw no sign of Arnold and walked over to the driver's seat. Then he saw the frog on the driver's seat gazing up at him forlornly. Arnold's lunch spread out next to it.

"Seamus, you're a cruel man," Finnian sighed. "Sorry, Mr Frog, I can't undo that man's cruel magic. So long to you" Finnian walked slowly along the New York streets. A few children pointed and laughed at him but mostly, he was not disturbed. Seamus O'Grady had recently escaped the prison he'd been condemned to and was now very angry and eager for revenge. There was a slight drizzle on that autumn day but Finnian didn't notice. Eventually, he walked into a clothing shop, and most people seemed unconcerned to see a three-foot man in funny clothes walking around in it. Finnian looked out the window, expecting to see Seamus go by at any moment. After half an hour with no sign of Seamus, he left the shop. A New York taxi was parked in front of him, it's rear door open with a potential customer talking to the driver. Finnian ran to the car and leapt into it. He'd found a large jacket in the clothes shop and used it to cover himself. He hadn't paid for it, so he hoped the car would leave soon. Eventually, the elderly woman sat in the back seat, and the car began to move. After a few minutes the woman asked the driver, a Mexican-looking man with a thick moustache.

"Excuse me, is this your coat on the back seat?"

"Is there a coat there?"

"Yes."

"Must be from my last passenger. Don't worry, I'll take it to lost property.

Finnian shook nervously, hoping the woman wouldn't lift up the coat. Eventually, the cab stopped, and Finnian heard the door open as she got out. He waited a few seconds, and the inevitable happened. The coat was lifted up by the driver, who saw the shaking leprechaun and gasped in surprise and disbelief.

"Thanks for the taxi ride. Here's a gold piece!" Finnian yelled at the driver and hurled the gold coin at him as he ran out past.

"Hey!" the driver called, but Finnian was long gone. The streets were getting dark now. The last ride had been a long one, and Finnian was relieved by the cover of darkness. He was terrified of the power that

Seamus had. Seamus was far more powerful than him and knew if he found Finnian, he'd be in big trouble. The rain was getting heavier. The streets were bright with neon signs and Finnian felt very alive and very scared. A dog leapt up at him and knocked him over, soaking his green suit in the gutter.

"Hey Gilbert, stop that! Sorry buddy," a young man called out.

Finnian picked himself up and wondered what to do with himself. He had incredible powers himself but couldn't use them in all situations.

"Mum, look at that funny little man," a young girl said, pointing at him.

"Don't be rude," her mother said, dragging her away.

Eventually, Finnian came across a cinema with a long queue outside. He wasn't one to watch films much. He'd seen Darby O'Gill and the little people but found it farfetched. He decided he'd go into the cinema and sleep in there for the night, hidden away. A few people in the queue looked at him as he approached and then he darted swiftly between their legs and dashed upstairs, grabbing some fallen popcorn on the way. He dashed past the usher at the cinema door, who yelled in dismay, and then he hid himself, gasping and wheezing under a row of seats. He expected people would be looking for him now, as well as the dreaded Seamus. He ate some of the popcorn, which was gone in five minutes.

People began to stream in, and Finnian had to find a spot where nobody was sitting. He didn't know if it was a popular blockbuster movie that would fill the picture house and he hoped it wouldn't fill completely. He ran to the front row and hid close to the wall. The front row was very close to the screen, and he hoped fewer people would watch from there.

Mumbling voices filled the arena, and eventually, the footsteps stopped. Nobody else was coming in. Music was playing. Not the kind of music that Finnian liked. After several minutes, the curtains opened, and adverts began to show.

"Oh, what is going to happen?" he whispered to himself.

More time passed. Finnian could see a few people were in the front row but not in the corner where he was hidden. The film began, and the audience was whooping and cheering in delight. Finnian couldn't see the screen from his hiding place, but after a few minutes something caught his attention that seemed a little odd. The voices on the screen had changed to a single voice. A voice that was familiar to him. He ventured from his hiding place to look at the screen himself.

"Finnian Coghlan, I'm coming to find you!" the voice yelled. Finnian looked at the cinema screen and saw the shape of Seamus O'Grady filling the entire screen. The crowd were whooping with delight, convinced it was part of the movie. "Oh my God," Finnian gasped.

"Aha, I see you. You little rascal" The huge figure on the screen gazed at his quarry and then the screen exploded as the tiny man burst out of it. He dropped into the aisle on the right side of the screen. Finnian was on the left side and he quickly ran out of the auditorium with the audience clapping and cheering the unusual spectacle. The screen was now black and torn and hung in strips from where Seamus had emerged. He ran after Finnian, but after a few steps, an audience member put out his foot to trip Seamus, and the little man stumbled to his knees.

"Why, you ugly beast!" Seamus yelled at him and held his hand out at him. The man laughed, but then there was a blinding flash of light, and he turned into a frog. His girlfriend next to him screamed, but the audience cheered more. This was the most entertaining film they'd ever seen.

Finnian ran out to the cinema. Someone saw him go and called out, "So you didn't like the film then?" but Finnian was too terrified to look back at who'd said it. Seamus followed seconds later. His face was as red as his suit. "What's so bad about the movie?" the same young man asked him. Seamus glared at the man who'd asked.

"Where did he go?" he yelled.

"Down there," the man pointed, and Seamus ran in the direction indicated.

Shops were beginning to close, but many remained open. Finnian ran into another clothes shop. Always good for a hiding place, but Seamus saw him and followed him into it.

"I'll get you, Finnan, you little scumbag!" he yelled. "You'll never hide from me."

Finnian ran upstairs, not waiting for the escalator, and Seamus carried on in pursuit. Eventually Finnian stopped in front of a huge mirror and watched as Seamus emerged from the escalator.

"OK, Seamus, you win," he said, gasping and wheezing. "I'm too old to run."

"Thought you could get away, did you?" Seamus snarled. "I'll make you pay for condemning me to the spirit world."

"You wanted to steal my gold," Finnian replied. "Well, now it's your turn to be condemned."

Seamus hollered, and a blast of light flew from his hand. Finnian dived out of the way, and the light struck the mirror and rebounded back to Seamus.

"Noooo!" Seamus screamed as the light engulfed him. There was a rainbow flash, and Seamus disappeared. A large green frog was there in his place.

Finnian got up and looked around. There weren't many shoppers on that floor, and nobody seemed to have witnessed this confrontation. He walked over to the frog and picked it up.

"They say all magic is done with mirrors, don't they, my little friend?" he said to the passive creature. "Don't worry. I'll take you to a pet shop or an aquarium where you can live out your froggy days."

Finnian laughed to himself and walked down the escalator, frog in hand.

A whimsical

19.

Cyril Mfede walked slowly off the pitch. It had been a bad half of football, and his team were 3-0 down. Although the weather was bright and sunny on a spring day in May, he couldn't have felt gloomier. He'd been playing for the under-11s team for 3 months. He'd scored 3 goals on his debut, but now the goals were drying up, and his manager grumbled about it. He walked alongside the watching parents; some had been clapping earlier, but he heard something that made him look up sharply.

"Oi son, want some of my banana?" Cyril saw a fat, pasty-faced man eating a banana with a horrible smirk on his face. As he looked at him, the man made a monkey noise and then threw back his head and laughed. Cyril scowled but did not react. He carried on walking. His teammates had already left the pitch and were now in the dressing room being undoubtedly roasted by the boss. He walked around the side of the building alone, sat on a metal can and put his head in his hands. He would probably have stayed there for the whole of half time when a voice suddenly caught his attention.

"Cheer up, m'lad," it said.

He looked up slowly and couldn't credit what he was seeing. A very short man, all dressed in green with a ginger beard and green hat. He looked old, and his accent was strongly Irish.

"Who are you?" Cyril asked.

"Just a passing bystander. My name is Finnian Coghlan, and I've come along to cheer you up."

"You can't do anything for me" Cyril replied and put his head back in his hands.

"Come now, don't underestimate the little people. I know what's been happening, and I think I can help."

"How can you help me?" Cyril asked without looking up. "I know what you've been going through as I've gone through the same myself."

Cyril shot him a fierce look. "You don't know what it's like. You're white."

"Ah, but I'm Irish, my young friend. I've had all kinds of abuse, which I won't trouble your ears with now. Pray, what is your name?"

"Cyril."

"I think I can help you, Cyril."

"Nobody can help!" Cyril shouted and looked at Finnian as if he was on the verge of tears." My dad said it was worse years ago, but it's still bad now, and I'm sick of it. I try really hard to be a good player, to show the people who abuse me what I can do, I just want to play football. I'm not bothering anyone. Why do they have to be like that?" He stood up. His lower lip was shaking.

"Please sit down, Cyril. I can help you, I promise," Cyril sat down, eyeing the man suspiciously. He couldn't credit seeing someone so short, but his thoughts were too consumed with his own problems to care about that. "I'm going to give you something. A present, Cyril, that will cost you nothing."

"Why? It's not my birthday. I'm not 11 until Christmas day."

"Then you can have a second birthday" and then Finnian sat on the floor and began taking off his shoes. They were gold-coloured, showing green socks underneath.

"Why are you doing that?" Cyril asked, perplexed. "I'm giving you my magic boots," Finnian replied with a grin.

"They won't fit me, and they've got no studs on them."

"Aha," Finnian replied.

"Watch" Cyril sat in awe as the boots were surrounded by golden light, expanding in size until they were the same size as his current boots.

"Take your boots off and put these on," Finnian insisted.

"You're weird," Cyril replied. "How do you do things like that?"

He looked around the deserted alley nervously. His team and coach would be wondering where he was. Maybe he'd be substituted before the second half.

"You don't have much time," Finnian insisted. "Please hurry."

Suspiciously, Cyril undid his boots, took them off and tried the golden-coloured ones the strange man had given him. They fit perfectly and were light and comfortable. He noticed they had studs underneath. He stood up and paced up and down a bit. He felt like he was gliding over the ground rather than walking on it.

"They feel great," he said.

"What about my old boots?"

"You won't need them," his friend answered. "But my dad bought me those. He'll wonder what I did with them."

"Let him wonder. Believe me, you won't be missing them" "OK, I'll trust you," answered Cyril and gave a nervous sigh. "I'd better go and see the others before I get into trouble."

"May the luck of the Irish go with you," replied the little man, and he gave a bow, removing his hat briefly as he did so.

"Whatever, but thanks anyway," Cyril said and walked back to the dressing room. His manager was predictably berating his team, and as he walked in, the yell of.

"Where have you been?" was hurled at him.

"Sorry, I needed time alone," Cyril answered. He sat down and waited for the halftime break to be over. Eventually, it was, and the team returned to the field. Cyril saw the goalkeeper of the other team, West Ham, talking to the horrible fat man who'd abused him at halftime. He knew the boy's name was Daniel Jason, and he suspected the man was his father. He was a stocky boy with a blonde crew cut and shot Cyril a filthy look as he returned to the pitch. As ever, Cyril didn't react. He wanted his football to do the talking, and hopefully, now he could do just that.

Cyril's team, Hackney, had just 30 minutes to turn the game around. They were nearing the end of the season and were two points behind their rivals, who led the table. A win today would put Hackney on top of the league with just one game to go. Cyril felt determined. He looked around at the parents and saw his dad standing some way from the others. He gave Cyril the thumbs up as the teams returned to their positions.

The ref blew his whistle, and the ball was passed to Cyril. He ran a few steps with the ball and was alarmed by the sudden acceleration in his feet, but he didn't lose control of the ball and found himself seconds later one-on-one with the goalie. Daniel Jason in goal eyed him and mouthed a slur that Cyril didn't quite pick up, but instinct made him take a quick shot, and the ball looped over Daniel's head and smashed into the bottom corner. Cyril stopped and gasped. He'd never looped a goal like that before, and his teammates quickly surrounded him to celebrate his goal.

Cyril saw his dad cheering and then noticed something odd above his dad's head. It was the little man in green, and he seemed to be tied to several balloons that were keeping him afloat. He was also clapping in delight. Unable to believe what he was seeing, he looked away and readied himself for the restart. West Ham kicked off, and a large Indian boy ran into Cyril, knocking him over. Cyril got up quickly, unfazed and went in for the tackle. He won the ball cleanly, and it squirted over to his friend Alf, who ran towards the opponent's goal. The defender forced a corner, and Cyril volunteered to take it. Cyril was left-footed and this would be an inswinger. He suspected what would happen but was no less delighted when it did. The ball curled into the top corner past the goalkeeper's despairing dive, and once again, a huge cheer went up.

Even some opponents were applauding. Daniel picked up the ball and glared at Cyril. He made a cutting motion across his neck. Cyril wasn't scared as he'd faced bullies before and knew he was going to get the upper hand on this one. The next few minutes were scrappy. A lot of throw-ins and a few free kicks, but Cyril knew when he got the ball again, he'd make something happen. With ten minutes to go, he got his chance. A defensive mix-up while Cyril had his back to goal, and the ball was dropping from a height. He then did something that had never worked before: an overhead kick. The ball was struck true and smashed into the goal with too much power for anyone to stop it. It was 3-3! Hackney was back in it. Again, the game resumed, and with five minutes left, it seemed like it would finish a draw. Cyril felt an extreme energy. He knew his team could win this, and eventually, he found himself on one with the goalkeeper. As Cyril dinked the ball in the air, Daniel dived at Cyril's feet, knocking him to the ground.

"Penalty!" his team shouted in unison. Daniel got up, swore and shouted, "That's not a penalty," The referee blew his whistle and pointed to the spot.

"You can't do this!" Daniel shouted at the ref. "Any more dissent, and you're off," the ref warned. He was a middle aged, balding and slightly overweight man. He looked out of breath, but he knew the rules, and that was a penalty. Cyril picked up the ball and grinned at Daniel who spat on the ground defiantly. As Cyril lined up his kick, he could see fear in his opponent's eyes. He knew he would score. He had enchanted boots. Something he wouldn't have believed possible but was happening nonetheless. He ran to the ball, struck it, and it shot into the middle of the goal, striking Daniel in the crotch. Daniel fell to the ground in agony, and the ball trickled underneath him into the net. It was 4-3, and Cyril had got all 4 goals.

The cheer was huge. The watching parents were clapping and cheering. His dad was punching the air. Daniel's dad was shouting at the referee at the side of the pitch. Eventually, the game restarted, but after a few minutes, the final whistle went and Cyril's dad ran joyfully to his son.

"That was amazing, son," he called happily. "I always knew you had it in you."

"I had some help," Cyril replied. He pointed to his boots and laughed.

"Where did you get those boots?" his dad asked, then after a pause, said, "Oh, but who cares? You're a hero. Your mum will be so proud when I tell her," Cyril's dad drove them back after the match. Cyril was sat in the back seat looking out of the window when he noticed a movement in the seat next to him. He looked across and saw his mysterious benefactor in the car next to him. He was grinning with his thumbs up.

"Thanks, Finnian," he whispered, "That was the best day of my life."

"Sure and begorrah," the little man replied. "It is my job to make kids like you happy. Don't tell your dad where you got the boots, and they will bring you luck forever."

"Who are you talking to, Cyril?" his dad called. "Oh, just a friend, Dad," he smiled to himself, "A very good friend."

whimsicalCyil & n
Glorious Victory

20.

Dorothy Waterfield sat alone in her care home armchair. She had a room to herself and had just said goodbye to her son and daughter and the four children they had between them. She was 98, and had lived a full, long life and knew the end was near, but hopefully not too near, as she was currently watching her favourite film on the TV in the corner of her room. She'd seen Casablanca around forty times but never tired of it. This time, it was on TV, and as always, she was gripped. The nurse would be along in a couple of hours with her evening meal. Currently, she was sipping from a bottle of an energy drink her daughter had brought her. Sometimes, she fell asleep in her chair but felt very alert today. About halfway through the film, as Humphrey Bogart made one of his memorable monologues, something strange happened. The TV screen went completely white and stayed that way for over 30 seconds and she considered calling the nurse but froze as she saw something extraordinary.

A little man, all dressed in green, appeared in the middle of the screen. He wore a green top hat and had a ginger beard. He looked very old, but his eyes shone with youthful wisdom. He was grinning broadly.

"Top of the morning to you, Dot," he said in a crisp Irish accent.

Dorothy sat in silence. It wasn't the morning, but how did he know her name?

"Hello," she replied hoarsely and nervously. "Who are you? I was watching the film."

"I'm a figment of your imagination," he replied and then laughed hysterically. Dorothy felt a twinge of unease.

"How are you in my television?" she asked. "How can you see me from in there?"

"Oh, I can do miracles, Mrs Waterfield," he replied happily. "I'm a five-thousand-year-old leprechaun from Glendalough."

Dorothy was speechless and a little scared. She decided she'd call for the nurse. She pressed the button and waited. While she waited, the man in green on the white background faded away, and her film carried on. A minute later, the nurse, a Portuguese woman in her 30s, came into the room.

"Is something wrong, Mrs Waterfield?" she asked.

"There was something funny on the TV," she replied.

The nurse, called Adriana looked at the screen. "It's just an old film. Do you want me to turn it off for you?"

"No, it doesn't matter. I saw a little man in green on the TV. He looked like a leprechaun and had an Irish accent. I must have fallen asleep and dreamt it."

"OK, Mrs Waterfield, if there's no other problem, I will leave you to your film."

"Thank you, nurse," Dot replied.

Adriana left, and for five minutes, nothing else happened. It was starting to rain outside, and the film was nearing its conclusion.

"Top of the day to you!" a little voice said. This time, to her left. She looked to the left at her cupboard of clothes where the voice had come from. The cupboard was closed. What was going on? She watched, holding her breath a bit, as a tiny hand emerged from the door and opened it with a faint squeal. She recoiled as the little man emerged into her room.

"Who are you ?" she called in horror. "How did you get in here? Am I dreaming again?"

"You're only dreaming if it's a dream come true," he replied, and he tottered into the room, his little feet faintly audible on the carpet.

"Now to business," he went on. "I'm a very old man. Older than any person you've seen in your life, and I think I can do something amazing for you."

"Will you give me gold from the end of a rainbow?" she asked, almost laughing.

"Oh no, and don't interrupt. It's something far better "He tottered over to the TV and picked up a photograph that was next to it. It was a photograph of Dorothy and her late husband Herbert on their wedding day 65 years ago. Herbert had been dead for eight years, and the grief had contributed to her decline and need for care.

"This is you and your husband, isn't it?" he asked her. "How young and beautiful you are."

She relaxed slightly. "Yes, a lot of men were after me back then," she said happily.

"But my Herbert was always the one I wanted. We had a wonderful time together and travelled all around the world. We had a wonderful family and... oh, how I miss him," she began to cry a little. "Are you really a leprechaun?"

"Indeed I am. The finest in the world. My name is Finnian Coghlan, and I was born in Ireland, although I do most of my business in England."

"What sort of business?"

"Miracles mainly, and sorting out people's problems."

"Then why have I never heard of you before?"

"Because," he hissed, "I swear them to secrecy; otherwise, terrible luck will befall them if they betray my word."

"Gosh" she answered, and after a pause. "So what do you want to do for me?"

He looked at her thoughtfully, and she began to feel uneasy. She began to consider calling the nurse again but then he leapt in the air and howled. "I'm going to make you young again!"

"Don't be so ridiculous, you silly little man. I'm nearly done with this life. This must be a dream, or am I hallucin..." but before she could finish the word, Finnian leapt onto her lap and grabbed at her hair with both of his hands. She screamed and almost fell out of her chair. She felt a strange sensation going through her body and tried to push the leprechaun away.

"What are you doing?" she yelped and tried to stand up. At that point Finnian slithered to the ground and crawled over to the bathroom in the corner.

"Look what I've done for you," he yelled. "Look in the mirror."

Dorothy got to her feet and did so very quickly. Quicker than she had for decades.

"What the..." her hands went to her face. Her skin felt smooth and wrinkle-free. She walked quickly over to the bathroom, where Finnian hopped into the bathtub, giggling hysterically. She looked in the mirror above the sink and screamed again.

This time, even louder, "What's happened?" she cried at her reflection. Now she looked exactly as she had in her wedding photograph.

"The scream will alert the nurse," Finnian said, "so I'm out of here." He ran out of the bathroom, and Dorothy heard the cupboard for her clothes opening and closing on its squealing hinges. She heard more running feet, and the door to her room opened. One of the male attendants, a stocky man called Clive, came into the bathroom.

"Who was screaming?" he asked her. "Where is Dorothy?"

She looked at him. Her eyes widened, and she screamed. "I'm Dorothy! Something just happened to me."

"What on Earth? Explain who you are, or I may call the police."

"I'm Dorothy!" she screamed again. "I was made young again by a... by..." Then she remembered the leprechaun's words about being sworn to secrecy. "It's like something from a movie" she went on, gazing at her youthful face in the mirror.

"You do look like Dorothy," Clive said. "I don't believe you are her."

At that point, she reached out and slapped the man in the face.

"Don't call me a liar," she yelled.

"Then what happened, for God's sake? Do I call the Pope and tell him a miracle happened?"

"Don't call anyone. I'm going home," she muttered and walked out of the bathroom and sat in her chair holding her head in her hands.

Finnian, hidden in the closet, chuckled merrily away. Clive heard the laugh and walked to the cupboard door.

"Who is in there?" he demanded. No reply, so he tried to pull the door open, but it was held fast. "Dorothy, are you in there?" he added. "Something is going on, and I need you to explain who this young woman is. Please, Dorothy, I think you need help."

Young Dorothy got up, ignoring Clive and began packing her belongings in a bag her family had brought her. She was still wearing the old lady's nightgown and realised she needed to change out of it.

"If you don't tell me what's happening, I will call the police," Clive snapped at her.

Dorothy continued to ignore him and took her bagged change of clothes into the bathroom.

"Have you locked the old lady in this cupboard?"

She closed the bathroom door and began to get changed into better clothes.

"Right, that's it," Clive said and pulled out his mobile phone. No sooner had he done so than the cupboard door swung open and knocked the phone out of Clive's hand. It fell to the floor, and Clive stumbled, which made him tread on his phone, breaking it instantly. Finnian ran out of the cupboard laughing.

"Hey, what the..." Clive exclaimed. At this point, other staff members came into the room, alerted by the commotion. The little leprechaun ran between their legs and out into the corridor.

"What was that?" Adriana asked Clive. "What happened to Dot?"

The bathroom door opened, and young Dorothy stepped out in her going-out clothes. She walked past the stunned group without a word and left the room.

"Don't let her go," Clive yelled. "She's done something to Mrs Waterfield."

"I'll call the police," Adriana said and pulled out her own phone. As the phone rang, she asked. "What do I say to them?"

"An old lady has gone missing, and a young woman may know something. I'm going after her."

With that, he left the room to pursue the young Dorothy. He ran down the corridor, but there was no sign of her. Maybe she'd gone into a lift. They were on the second floor.

Dorothy was already out of the building. She was running and feeling hysterical. A miracle had been performed on her, but surely this was a dream. This never happened in the real world. The world she'd been used to for nearly a hundred years. She checked her purse and had a small amount of money. Maybe twenty pounds. Enough for a taxi. She got out her mobile phone, making sure she was out of sight of the care home and made a call. She hid behind a tree as Clive appeared briefly outside the front of the home. Eventually, he turned and walked back into it. A police car pulled up, and two officers got out. The phone her son had was ringing but he was not answering. He probably wasn't expecting her.

She decided to run for a bit, now that she could again, and she arrived at the church of latter-day saints that she'd been married in when she looked the way she seemed to look now. She leaned against a gravestone and decided to call for a taxi. She intended it to take her to her grandson's house nearby, but she stopped and thought for a while. Nobody would recognise her or believe her story. Her mental faculties weren't as sharp as in her youth, and she'd forgotten a lot of things that had happened in her life. She groaned and held her head where a migraine seemed to be developing.

"Everything OK?" a little voice chirped from behind a bush. Finnian poked his head out and grinned at her. "What do you think of my miracle?"

"I don't understand," she replied. "This can't be real. Things like this don't happen in the real world. Only in dreams and movies."

Finnian chuckled and walked towards her. She instantly stepped back until she was pressing against the side of the church.

"Please tell me what's happening" she gasped. "If you did this to me, then how and why did you do it?"

Finnian sighed and sat cross-legged on the ground in front of her.

"I'm a very old man," he said. "And very lonely. I do miracles to make friends, and so many of my friends grow old and die. After five thousand years, you see a lot of that, and it's heartbreaking, I can tell you."

She was breathing heavily. This was getting crazier by the minute.

"This may seem crazy," she said. "But I want you to make me back how I was. Aged 98. I can't deal with what you've done to me."

Finnian stood up and shrugged. "That's gratitude for you," he said. Then he clicked his fingers, turned his back and went back behind the bush.

Dorothy immediately fell to the ground. Her legs just gave way, and she twisted her ankle, which made her groan in pain. As she reached out to rub her ankle, she noticed her hand was aged and lined again. She fumbled for a phone to call an ambulance. She got through and told them of her location before she passed out.

When she regained consciousness, she was aware she was lying on a very comfortable bed, her left leg was aching, and she was vaguely aware of people standing around her.

"She's back." a voice said. Adriana's voice. "Are you OK, Mrs Waterfield? You gave us a nasty scare there."

"It was a dream," she murmured in reply. "It must have been a dream. Her vision was becoming clearer and she realised she was back in her room at the care home.

"Your ankle is badly twisted, but otherwise, you're OK." She heard Clive's voice say.

The staff helped her sit up gradually, and she saw her children and grandchildren watching anxiously from the end of the bed.

"Did you see the little man? Where is he? The leprechaun."

"She may be feverish," Clive said as he turned to her family. "I've no idea how she got to the church. Somebody must have taken her there."

"The little man called Finnian," she repeated. "All in green."

"Just try and rest now," Adriana said calmly. Dorothy closed her eyes. Then she opened them again.

"Can I have a mirror?" she snapped.

"What for?" asked Clive.

"Am I old again?"

"You're a very young 98 that puts us all to shame," he said with a smile. "Now, just try and sleep awhile, and I'll consult your family outside."

The group of people filed out of the room leaving her watching the TV in the corner of her room. As she watched, she saw the nature program on there begin to fade away and was replaced with an entirely white background. Her eyes widened as the little man appeared on the screen, chuckling and smiling. He gave her the thumbs up and then faded out of sight.

21.

Father Edward O'Halloran walked slowly to the altar in the old church. He'd been a father for seven years and knew everybody by heart who visited. Later that day a wedding was planned, and he came to see that everything was as it should be. He looked around, enjoying the silence until his eyes landed on a figure in the corner of the chapel. He was a small, green-suited figure in a green hat with large shoes. He appeared to be asleep, and father Edward walked to him in annoyance.

"Hey you!" he called. "This isn't a doss house. It's a place of God. Get out of here, please."

The little man sat up sharply, and green eyes pierced the father with a fierce-looking intelligence behind them.

"Oh, sorry, father," the little man replied in a thick Irish accent. "You see, I travel so much I forget where I am and will fall asleep anywhere. Didn't mean to trouble you." He took off his hat and scratched his bald head. "You're a man of the cloth, and there's some things I'd like to talk to you about while I'm here."

"Like what? I'm a busy man and have much to do later" "Surely that can wait awhile. I need to talk to you about Jesus."

The father sighed. "Well, that's why we're all here," he said. "Only so many people don't have faith any more it almost seems like a waste of time."

"Jesus a waste of time, Father? Surely not. I'm older than Jesus, don't you know? Five thousand years old, and I was born in Glendalough."

"What rubbish. Nobody is that old, and if you're a madman wasting my time, be off with you."

The little man leapt in the air, making the father recoil, and he landed on top of the altar. Then he sat down and crossed his legs.

"I must be dreaming," the vicar said. "You're such a tiny man, and you can do things like that."

"I can do miracles, Father," the little man said, grinning. "My name is Finnian Coghlan, and I want to change the world."

"Jesus already did that."

"Oh, but father, I've travelled the world. I speak two hundred languages and have met children of all faiths. Muslim. Hindu, Buddhist and Sikh, as well as what you preach."

"What are you trying to tell me?"

At that point, Finnian pulled out a small pipe. "You can't smoke in here!" the father snapped.

"OK, Father," and he put the pipe in a hidden pocket. "Look, father. The dreams of children are eternal, but childhood itself isn't, and I've seen the pain of so many youngsters in agony over the loss of it."

The vicar sat down in the front pew, raised his glasses and rubbed his eyes. He was an old man and not used to such situations. "Look, what is it you want?" he asked.

"I don't want anything, Father," Finnian replied. "I have everything I need. Don't you know the scientists tell us we're all going to die, then all the stars will burn out, and everything will be gone forever?"

"Well, Jesus said Heaven and Earth will pass away, but his words will never pass away."

"Yes, that's a bold statement," answered Finnian. "But if there's nobody around to register his words, is there a need for them?"

"Oh, I've heard all this secular claptrap before. I'm a man of faith, and nothing, and nobody will take it from me. You come from Ireland by the sound of it, which is famously a Catholic country, so do you have a faith?"

"My faith," Finnian replied mysteriously, "is the dreams of childhood, and it's they who make people like me exist."

"Yes, but childhood is very brief and the business of the church is mostly concerning funerals and weddings and connecting people to God in that way."

"Do you believe in magic, Father?"

"Magic is the devil."

"So you believe in the devil?"

"Well, of course, it's part of my faith."

"Do you believe I can do miracles?"

"Only the saints can do miracles."

Finnian leapt in the air, "Then I'm the saint Finnian Coghlan" he cried.

Father Edward stood from the pew and shook his head in disbelief. "Look, I don't know who you are or why you're trying to disrupt my day," he said, "but I think you're a man who probably needs help. The mental health services are very good in England."

At that point, Finnian leapt off the altar and ran into a corner of the church, where he quickly reappeared with a white candle. He held it up to Father O'Halloran. "Look at this, Father," he hissed, his eyes dancing with delight. At that point, there was a bright white flash, and the candle changed colour to gold.

"What on Earth..." the father leapt back in shock. "Look, I don't know what your game is, but I may have to call the police if you don't leave this chapel."

"Come now, Father, you believe in miracles, so look what I've done here". He dropped the gold candle to the ground which made a very solid noise, more metallic than the sound of a candle.

"Despite his fear, which made him very tetchy at this peculiar intruder, the father walked towards the object and picked it up. It felt and looked like gold. How was this possible?

"Good grief," he murmured. "How on Earth did you do that?"

"The same way Jesus turned water into wine" "Really?" the vicar said, staring at the gold lump in his hand that was once a candle. "With powers like that you really could change the world. What else can you do?"

The church cleaner had entered by a side door. She saw the father talking and supposed he was praying. She didn't see Finnian. After a moment's thought, she decided to leave him on his own with his God.

"What can I do, father?" Finnian replied slowly and steadily, "It brings all the world's faiths together and unites the human race."

"Such a thing is impossible, although it's a lovely thought," Father O'Halloran replied. Then his face changed, and he looked up. "But maybe you're a conjurer or trickster. I've seen sleight of hand magic, and it's all fake. How can I believe you're capable of miracles?"

"The miracle is childhood, Father," Finnian said with a slow grin. "It's the reason the universe exists."

"Well, Jesus said you become like children to receive the kingdom of Heaven."

"So, we've agreed on that then."

"I suppose so," and the father sat down with a sigh.

"Look, I'm very old and too much excitement isn't good for me. I respect that you're a man with a good heart, and I don't know if you really changed a candle to a piece of gold, but I'm very tired now and need to prepare for a wedding later today."

"OK, Father, thanks for your time. I'll be gone now, but remember this one thing. It's all about the little people."

There was a bright flash of rainbow-coloured light, and he was gone.

22.

It was Christmas morning, about 6:30 am when Paul and Stephanie decided to creep downstairs to open their presents under the huge tree that had been put up. The twins were excited, convinced they'd see Father Christmas place them there as they tiptoed downstairs. Paul got to the presents first. Their parents were asleep upstairs and they wanted to enjoy what they found without them knowing just yet. Paul picked up a small box, tore it open and was delighted at the large toy car within. It had a remote control with batteries supplied. Stephanie decided to separate her presents before opening them and she saw that she'd had ten presents from grandparents, aunts and uncles as well as her parents. A very large present without a label mysteriously leaned against the tree stump. It was covered in patterned green paper and seemed to be making a strange noise. Almost like a person snoring.

Within an hour the children had opened all their presents, whispering to each other in delight at what they'd received, but both were curious about the big green present that seemed to have appeared overnight. They were sure it wasn't there before. Eventually, curiosity became too much for them, and the children both tried to lift the present. It was exceptionally heavy and made odd thudding sounds when they moved it.

"I'm sure something moved by itself inside," Paul whispered to his sister.

"Let's get it open," she answered, her eyes wide with excitement. " Maybe this one is from Father Christmas himself. "

They pulled the large box, for that's what it felt like it was into the middle of the room and were about to tear the paper off when footsteps on the stairs were noticeable.

"Oh, hello, kids. Merry Christmas," their mother said tiredly. "I've been drinking too much lately. Had too much last night and don't feel like getting up yet. I'm just getting a glass of water. Have you had a lot of nice presents?"

"Oh yes, mummy, thank you," Stephanie said in delight.

"But what's this big one?" Paul cut in. "Who is it from, and who is it for?"

Their mother gave a groan. "OH, I don't know. It was on the doorstep outside yesterday and your father brought it in. It was very heavy and we supposed it was from the neighbours. I expect it's a big box of beers or something for your father. He had a lot last night as well and won't be up for hours.

The children looked excitedly at each other. They wanted to see what the strange present was. Their mother got her glass of water from the kitchen and trudged slowly back to bed. They heard the bed creak as she settled back and both began tearing at the beautiful green paper. Surely it was something better than boring beer. Once the paper was off they saw a large white wooden box with a picture of a four leafed clover on the front of it. Paul was about to lift the lid on the box when Stephanie put a hand out to stop him.

"Wait," she hissed.

"What is it?" he replied impatiently.

"Sound like a man snoring. Listen. "The children stopped and quietly listened.

"Probably dad snoring," Paul went on and grabbed at the box.

"No, it's coming from inside the box," Stephanie insisted.

"Then let's find out what it is," Paul replied and pulled at the lid of the box. The hinges squeaked as it opened, and what the children saw made them both leap back in surprise. The box lid slammed shut. The children began breathing quickly, their hearts hammering, and they wondered if their parents would investigate the noise. After a minute, they realised that they wouldn't and decided to discuss what they'd seen.

"A little man sleeping in a box," Paul gasped. "Should we tell our parents?"

Before Stephanie could answer, the box swung open, and the little man inside sat up and scratched his head. He was all dressed in green with a ginger beard and a top hat. He looked at the children, who stepped back in alarm.

"Don't be afraid, little ones," the man said in an Irish accent. "I'm Finnian Coghlan from Glendalough and I've brought you something special this Christmas."

"How did you get in there?" Paul asked slowly.

"One of my many miracles enables me to do all sorts of things, I can assure you," answered the little man gingerly, stepping out of the box.

"No wonder the box was so heavy," Stephanie commented. She felt nervous at her boldness to speak.

"Oh, I'm not that heavy, really. Must be my heavy clothes. Now, what three wishes do you want me to grant you?" The children stared at him in surprise.

"Have you forgotten how to speak?" he went on. "That's my Christmas miracle for you."

"We never believed such things could happen," Paul answered.

"But you believe in Father Christmas surely. Come now, the pair of you are only eight years old. "

The children gasped.

"How did you know that?" asked Stephanie, her lips quivering.

"This is amazing!" Paul yelled excitedly. "He's a leprechaun from Ireland come to grant us miracles. Maybe he'll bring us a pot of gold, and we'll all be rich. Oh, I can't believe it. I can't believe it," and Paul began to jump in excitement while Finnian and Stephanie watched him silently.

"Oh, I wish you'd shut up," his sister said in annoyance.

"Your wish is granted, little girl," said the leprechaun. Paul stopped leaping and was mouthing words to his sister but she couldn't hear him.

"You've got two wishes left," Finnian said to Stephanie, who gasped. "I didn't mean to wish that. Does that mean he can't speak any more? "

"The only person who can hear him is himself," Finnian replied. Paul ran to his sister and grabbed her around the shoulders. His mouth was forming words, but she couldn't hear them. "Can he hear me?" she asked the leprechaun.

"Oh, absolutely, unless you wish him not to."

"Can I take back my wish?"

"Only if you waste another wish to make him talk again. "

Before she thought of gold, miracles and all manner of otherwordly exciting things, Stephanie said, "I wish I could hear you talk again."

". . . . now can you believe this? It's amazing. I can't believe it," Paul jabbered on in his familiar south London accent.

"Paul, stop and listen!" Stephanie yelled. Her brother went quiet. "We've just wasted two wishes and only have one wish left. "

Paul stopped and then sat down in an armchair. "How did we do that?" he asked.

"I made a wish that you couldn't talk and then wished you could," she said, with Finnian nodding in affirmation.

"Aye, that's what happened," he told Paul in his Irish lilt.

"Really?" Paul said, and before his sister could reply, he shouted in excitement, "Well, I wish we had a big Ferrari outside like all the rich people have."

"Your wish is granted," Finnian said quietly. "Now you've had your three wishes, I've nothing more to give you. "

"Oh Paul, you idiot, you've wasted something amazing. Think of all the things we could have done," but before Stephanie could say any more, Paul ran to the front door and looked outside. Lo and behold, a huge red Ferrari stood in the driveway, which Paul's dad had dreamt of his whole life.

"You did it!" Paul yelled at Finnian in delight. "My dad will be over the moon."

"Indeed he will," Finnian replied from the living room, standing in the same spot he'd stood in the whole time. The children realised how much taller they were than him. He was a full-grown man of about three feet in height. Stephanie joined her brother and looked at the car. "Isn't it incredible sis?" Paul asked her excitedly. "What else can the leprechaun do?" Finnian stood next to them. "I'm afraid you've used all three wishes, so I'll be going now. Enjoy your car, though."

The children looked at him. "Really, where are you going?" Stephanie asked.

"Somewhere to spend Christmas," he answered, and before they could reply, he ran down the driveway and disappeared around the corner. His tiny shoes were skittering on the stone floor.

"Oh well, Paul. Do we tell our dad the good news straight away? "

Paul wasn't listening. He was admiring the car and examining it from every angle. He loved cars, and this was the best one he'd ever seen. "The keys are in the door!" he yelled happily.

"Let's go and tell Dad."

"Oh really," she scoffed, "And how are we going to tell him we got this car?"

\Paul ignored her question and dashed back into the house with his feet pounding upstairs to his parent's room. Stephanie followed slowly, scratching her head.

"Mum! Dad! Get up! A leprechaun has given us a Ferrari for Christmas."

Stephanie heard her parents groaning in disbelief as they tried to deal with their Christmas Eve hangovers.

"What are you talking about, Paul?" their father said tiredly.

"Come down and see. It's in the driveway" Paul pounded down the stairs past his sister and out to the car. His father followed slowly in his dressing gown. It was cold and dark and he didn't need this, even on Christmas day. Stephanie followed them outside.

"Well, Dad, what do you think?" Paul asked as the three of them stood at the front door.

"How on Earth did that get here?" their dad asked.

"Chris, what's happened?" their mother said, following behind.

"The children say this car appeared somehow," he replied.

"That's a nice car," she said, "Looks like it's worth a fortune."

"The leprechaun did it!" Paul exclaimed. "It granted us a wish. "

"He granted us three wishes," his sister cut in, "but we wasted two of them."

"Don't talk nonsense," their mother said, opening the car door and looking inside. "It must be a prank by one of the neighbours. "

"Where did the leprechaun go, sis?" Paul said, turning to his sister. "He can tell them the truth. "

"He ran away after we used our three wishes," she answered forlornly.

"It's a beautiful car," their dad said, "Just what I always wanted, and brand new. Unusual number plate."

The four of them looked at the number plate. It just said FC1.

"I think that's the leprechaun's initials," Stephanie laughed.

"Look, please stop all this nonsense about such things," their mother cut in, "Tell us the truth. What do you know about this?"

The children looked at her in silence. They realised they could not convince their parents what had really happened.

"Let's go inside where it's not so cold," their father said. "And I want to know the truth of what has happened to you children, please. "

The four of them sat in silence in the living room. Their parents were holding mugs of coffee while the children looked sadly at all the torn wrapping paper on the floor. Eventually, Paul ran to the white box with the four-leafed clover on the front.

"The leprechaun was sleeping in this box," he told them, "We heard him snoring. "

"That's the strange heavy present we thought was from the neighbours, Chris," their mother said. "I wondered what it was. Now, children, there is no such thing as leprechauns. I'm very disappointed with you for causing all this upheaval at Christmas."

"He gave us three wishes, Mum," Stephanie replied. "I wasted two of them, and then Paul wished for a car for Dad."

"So it appeared outside," their dad said, "Sounds an amazing story. I'll take the car for a drive later. I still think it's probably my brother who brought it around, and you kids are letting your imaginations run away with you. "

"Kevin can't afford a car like that," their mother answered.

"Somebody put the car there, Trish."

"Whatever. I'm going back to bed. I've got a terrible headache. Now you kids play nice, and no more silly stories to us, please."

Their mother walked away to the stairs. Their father looked at the car keys his son had handed to him. "It looks legit," he said, "Later, I will take it out for a spin, but you kids are staying here. "

"OK, Dad," they said, disappointed that their little adventure hadn't been met with belief in their story. After their dad went upstairs, the kids gathered together all the torn paper from their presents and stuffed it in the kitchen bin. They weren't interested in their presents now that they'd seen this bizarre little man. They wondered if he'd turn up again and talked excitedly about the prospect of it. "Maybe he'll get us a pot of gold, sis."

"Maybe he'll grant us three more wishes," she replied.

While they were talking excitedly they didn't hear the footsteps tapping lightly on the kitchen floor and the sound of the catflap even though they no longer had a cat. The leprechaun came right up to them without them knowing and then hailed them heartily.

"Good day to you young children," he said. The children jumped in astonishment.

"Oh, Finnian, our parents don't believe in you," Stephanie cried. "I'll go and tell them your back."

She ran to the stairs, but Finnian held out her hand, and she froze in her tracks.

"What have you done? I can't move," she said.

"Hey, leave my sister alone," Paul called out. "Don't use magic on her." Finnian pulled his hand away, and she dropped to the floor.

"How did you do that?" she exclaimed.

"You mustn't let your parents see me," he replied. "If you do, the wish will be undone."

"But it's only a car," Stephanie answered. "We could have wished for something so much better than that."

"It was me who wished for that," Paul said. "Our dad won't believe our story that you made the Ferrari appear. He probably thinks we're mad."

Finnian leapt onto an armchair and sat down. "Sorry, children, I gave you three wishes, and you used all three," he said. "Perhaps you'll know to appreciate such things better next time."

"But really, who are you, and what do you want?" Stephanie asked.

"I'm a miracle worker from Glendalough in Ireland. I'm five thousand years old, and my name is Finnian Coghlan. I travel the world performing miracles and granting wishes. Today, I chose you people, but it will be someone else another day. "

"That's amazing," she replied. "Can grown-ups see you?"

"Only if I want them to," he went on. "The majority have closed their minds to people like me. They believe in life's cold and hard facts, especially money, above everything else. They wage wars against each other and cause a lot of unnecessary pain. I'm here to try and put things right, but we little people can only do so much. Today, I gave you a car with the power of my miracles but I could have got you anything if you hadn't wasted your wishes."

"So what will you do now?" she asked.

"I will be departing for other places, seeing other people all around the world."

"I wish we could go with you," Paul said.

"Unfortunately, your three wishes are gone," Finnian answered. "The moral of the story is to look before you leap and make sure you know you are equipped to deal with what is presented to you. I'll be going now, and you won't see me again, but next time, consider your life choices more carefully."

With that, he leapt off the chair and ran through the kitchen and out through the cat flap. He was gone.

23.

Nine-year-old Stan Smith was walking home from school. He'd had a bad day with the teacher calling him an idiot in front of the whole class when he couldn't remember his six times table. It was drizzling slightly and he pulled up the hood on his jacket. As he was passing a red letter box, there was a flash of orange light in front of him, which made him step back in surprise, almost tripping over a discarded tin can. A small man in a green suit and green top hat appeared in front of him.

"Don't look so surprised," said the little man in a strong Irish accent. "I'm Finnian Coghlan, and I'm here to make you rich. "

"I'm not supposed to talk to strangers," replied Stan. "My parents said so. "

"Very wise of your parents," replied Finnian. "But I'm not that strange, and I'm sure your parents would like you to be rich. "

Stan paused and looked at the odd man. There were other people on the pavement walking silently by,completely oblivious to the person he

was talking to. Maybe they couldn't see him. Maybe this was just a dream. "I need to get home and have my dinner," said Stan. "Don't hold me up.
"

At that point, Finnian held out his right hand. There was another flash of orange light, and an object appeared in it that looked like Stan's unfinished cheese sandwich he'd been given for lunch. "You didn't finish your sandwich," said Finnian.

"How did you get that out of my bag?" exclaimed Stan. He could see his teeth marks on the bread, which he gave up on as it was a bit stale.

"I can do miracles, my lad," said Finnian, grinning broadly. He had a thick ginger beard that glistened in the light. "Now I can do an even better one. "

He threw the sandwich into the air. Another flash of light, which was multicoloured and a lump of what looked like gold appeared in the little man's hand.

Stan gasped. "Is that what I think it is?" he asked Finnian.

"If you think it's gold, you'd be right, my young friend."

"Solid gold?"

"Worth a small fortune, and I'm giving it to you on one condition."

"What's that?"

"You don't tell your parents you have it. If you do, the magic will disappear, and it becomes a stale sandwich again."

Stan shrugged. "OK," he said and took it.

"Fantastic!" yelled Finnian, and he pirouetted with joy and then disappeared in a flash of orange light.

Stan gasped again and then looked down at the object the little man had given him. It was fairly heavy, so he stashed it in his school bag. The rain was getting heavier, so he quickened his pace for home. He didn't live far from the school, a ten-minute walk, but the rain often got him wet in seconds, and he urgently wanted his dinner.

That evening Stan lay in bed. He was an only child, so he had peace and quiet by himself quite often. He could hear his parents snoring in the other room, but he couldn't sleep due to his strange encounter on the way home from school. It was a Friday night, so he was off school for two days. At about ten in the evening, he was about to drop off when he heard a tap on his bedroom window. The curtain was drawn, and he pulled it back to find out what it was. He half suspected what he'd see but still jumped a little at the small, grinning man in his green suit and hat. Finnian was clinging to the branch of a tree that stood next to his window.

"Hello again," he called happily to the boy.

"What do you want from me?" Stan asked wearily. "It's late and I'm tired."

"I just wanted to thank you for keeping your promise of not telling your parents about the gold."

"How would you know if I did?"

"Aha. Leprechaun ingenuity," the man chuckled, touching his nose.

"Do you know everything I'm doing?"

"I'm thousands of years old," was the odd answer. "I'm full of the wisdom of the ancients and we people know a lot of things. "

Stan yawned. "Look, I'm very tired," he said. "Don't you ever sleep?"

"Only when I don't have important business."

"So I'm your business."

"At the moment, yes. I flew over from Ireland, from Glendalough south of Dublin, to find the right child to understand me."

"Why do I need to understand you?" Stan rubbed his forehead. He was getting a headache.

"Oh, I'm very lonely," Finnian replied, and his smile faded. He closed his eyes briefly and then looked down. His left arm was clinging to the branch with superhuman strength. "I will talk to you in the morning," he said with a sigh. "Keep the gold hidden from your parents, or it will turn back into a half-eaten sandwich. "

Stan shrugged. "OK. "

A flash of white light and Finnian disappeared. Stan walked away, holding his head and managed a couple of hours of sleep. What was in store in the morning?

Stan and his parents sat in silence at the breakfast table. Stan was munching a bowl of cereal while his dad had a boiled egg and his mum's toast and marmalade. Stan's dad rarely spoke in the morning. He worked long hours as a lorry driver and was often gone for days. His name was Peter, and he was bald and wore glasses. His mum, Christine had blonde hair, slightly greying and also wore glasses. Stan didn't wear glasses and was glad as a child in his class did, and he got bullied over it. Stan was sick of the bullies. He hoped Finnian would help him with their upsetting behaviour sometimes. He couldn't stop thinking about his new friend. He felt an excitement about this magical person and felt very lucky to have met him.

Eventually, Peter finished his egg, mumbled a few words to his wife and left the house, slamming the door slightly. Stan's mum finished her toast, looked at Stan and smiled. "What will you be doing today?" she asked him.

"Oh, this and that, "Stan replied. He really loved his mum and hated lying to her. He wanted to keep his promise to Finnian so he wouldn't say too much to his mum, who worked as a school dinner lady but not at his school. "Maybe I'll play some computer games."

At that moment, his mum's phone rang, and she whipped it out and spoke for a few minutes. She turned to her son and said. "OK, Stan, do as you please. I'm going out to see Jenny as she needs help in the garden. Love you, darling. "She got ready to leave the house.

Jenny was Christine's sister and was a twenty-minute drive away, so that Stan wouldn't be seeing his mum for a while. He'd be alone in the house, but would Finnian appear again? Stan trudged up the stairs to his room. He had a lot of computer games and a lot of books but didn't feel like either today. He really wanted to see Finnian, not just for the gold but he wanted to see if the little man could do other miracles. Stan's family weren't religious and never went to church, but like most people, they celebrated Christmas. That was months ago, and it was now the spring. The sun was shining. His clock said half past nine in the morning and he sat in his room looking at the window where he last saw the leprechaun. Would something exciting happen today?

Stan waited in his room for a couple of hours. He felt too excited to do any reading or play a computer game. His mum had texted him to say she'd be home in the evening. His dad was probably out working. He had hidden his lump of gold in a shoebox under his bed. He got it out to have a look at it. It was small and oblong like his sandwich had been. Why had Finnian given it to him? What would he do with it?

The weather clouded over, and a few light drops of rain struck the bedroom window. Perhaps his new friend wouldn't show up after all. He gave a groan and slumped onto his bed. Then he heard something.

"Hello there!" A cheerful Irish voice.

Stan sat up quickly. The voice had come from under his bed. Then he saw the little man roll out across the floor, grinning happily.

"How did you get in here?" exclaimed Stan

"The same way I travelled to England on a rainbow on St Patrick's Day," Finnian chuckled. "I can do miracles."

"Really?"

"I can solve all your problems. My power is limitless."

"That's very kind of you, but I'm sure there are a lot of kids worse off than me. Don't you want to help them?"

Finnian sat cross-legged on the floor with a serious look on his face. "That's a good point," he said.

Stan scratched his head. "I'm glad you chose me to be interested in. I'm a bit lonely too, how you say you are, but I don't come from a poor family and don't really need your gold. "

"Everyone needs gold," Finnian replied. "Why did I choose you? Why is anyone in the world chosen for anything? Some people get lucky."

"This is like meeting Father Christmas," Stan exclaimed.

"Oh, he works harder than me," replied the little man. "But there is one thing I like about you, and that's your language. "

"What do you mean, language?"

"You don't talk like those awful kids with their horrible words. Clearly, they've been brought up very badly."

Stan stopped and thought. His parents never swore at him, and he didn't. He heard a lot of foul language from his classmates. Typical of 21st-century London, but he thought nothing of it much. It was just something he'd got used to.

"And you're not a bully," added Finnian. "I hate bullies. I've lived for five thousand years and seen a lot of bullying in that time."

Stan gasped. "Five thousand years! Really?"

Finnian shrugged. "Yes, and I've been very lonely in that time. So few people worthy of my attention."

He got up and paced silently up and down in Stan's room. "I want to change the world," he said eventually. "And I think you can help me."

Suddenly Stan's phone rang. Finnian leapt in surprise. "Don't worry," said Stan, picking up the phone from a chest of drawers. He looked at it. "It's only my dad. Hello dad. "

After a brief conversation, Stan put the phone down and said to Finnian. "My dad is going to be here in half an hour. He wants to cook us our dinner. "

Finnian then grabbed Stan's phone from his hand. Stan yelped in surprise, and the leprechaun threw it up in the air, and another flash of light came from it. Finnian caught it as it fell and grinned. It, too, had turned into a bar of gold.

"But that's my phone!" Stan protested. "I'll be needing that."

"Make your decision, my lad." Finnian grinned. "Do you want a phone or to be rich? Also, don't forget not a word to your dad."

Finnian walked over to Stan's wardrobe and stepped inside, closing the door behind him. Stan opened it, and his strange friend had gone. He gave a weary groan and looked at the new bar of gold on the floor. He placed it next to the other one in his shoebox and sat on his bed, holding his aching head.

Stan didn't know what to tell his dad as they ate dinner in silence. His parents were vegetarian, and they tucked into a cheese and leek pie. As they were finishing, Stan's mum came into the dining room. She looked very tired.

"Hello, my love, how is your sister?" his dad asked her.

"I left her sleeping on the settee," she replied.

"Want some dinner?"

"I ate over there. Stan, can I borrow your phone for a second, as I seem to have lost mine. I thought it was in the car but I can't find it anywhere. "

Stan gulped. "Who do you need to call?" he forced out.

"I just wanted to call my brother and tell him I forgot to buy his daughter the dress I'd promised her. "

"You can borrow mine," said his dad, holding it out to her.

Stan sighed with relief and made an excuse to go to his room. He had a lot to think about and needed to be alone. Stan didn't see Finnian on Sunday or during his whole week at school. Maybe he'd dreamt the whole thing, but he'd check the shoebox every evening and saw those two bars of gold he had no idea what to do with. He'd sit alone at school. Daydreaming and drawing sketches of Finnian Coghlan that he made sure his teachers and classmates didn't see.

It was his tenth birthday on the Monday following his week of not seeing the leprechaun. He wondered about his phone that had turned to gold. He told his mum he'd lost it at school, for which she scolded him and, as a punishment, wouldn't get him another one. Maybe she'd change her mind on his birthday. He was going to have a small party on the Sunday before, and about seven friends from school were invited. As a precaution he'd moved the two bars of gold to a dark corner at the back of his wardrobe where hopefully nobody, his friends or parents, would find them.

Stan's birthday was a lot of fun. He and his friends played a lot of games. They had cakes, and he got presents. Everyone had a good time and left him smiling and happy at his house with his parents, but he was always thinking of Finnian and his gold bars and when he'd see him again.

At the end of the day, he retired to bed with a sigh. His parents had bought him a new phone, and he would make sure he never got it out in front of the little man again. He put on his TV, saw nothing that interested him and turned it off, and then he heard a slight knocking from the inside of his wardrobe. Stan looked at the wardrobe and wondered what to do.

"Is that you, Finnian?" he asked, not too loudly, as his parents were not yet asleep.

"Sure and begorrah it is," replied a muffled voice. "I didn't think much of Narnia and so I left it. "

Stan laughed and opened the wardrobe door. "I've read all those books," he said as Finnian tumbled out and then leapt into the air, standing upright.

"Happy birthday, my boy," he said and bowed, removing his hat as he did so. "I suppose you will be wanting your present now."

"I got a lot of presents, I.... " He hesitated. He could hear his father coughing outside his room. His heart began beating fast. He was alarmed that his dad might open the door.

"Quick, hide," he whispered to Finnian.

Stan's bedroom door then swung open, and his father stood there in his dressing gown. Stan gasped and glanced at Finnian, who stood unmoved and grinning broadly.

"Were you talking to someone?" his father asked sternly.

Stan gulped, and Finnian remained where he was. "I er.. erm," was all Stan could respond with.

"I don't want you losing your phone again, Stan," his father went on. "And close your wardrobe door. Now, goodnight."

With that, he closed the door, and Stan realised straight away that Finnian was invisible to his father.

Stan let out a huge breath. "He didn't see you. Why not?" he whispered to Finnian.

"It's a miracle, my lad," Finnian replied. "I do them all the time. "

"Would he be able to see my bars of gold if he looked in the box they're in?"

"Very much so," said Finnian. "That is why I don't want your parents to find them."

"They're well hidden," replied Stan. "That gave me a fright." He was still whispering as he didn't want his parents to hear him talk. They might send him to a child psychologist if they heard him talking to himself. He heard his parent's bed creaking as his dad returned to it.

"For your present from me," Finnian carried on, walking over to Stan's 30-inch TV and then tapping it lightly with his hand. "How about this?"

There was another huge flash of multicoloured light, and Stan's TV disappeared. It too had become a bar of gold-but an absolutely huge one! This lump of gold was the size of his TV. There was no way he could conceal it from his parents, and how could he explain that his TV had gone missing? After a while, he said, "Look, Finnian, I can't have a lump of gold that big. Plus, what do I tell my parents when they see my TV has gone?"

"Why don't you sell it before your parents find out?" was the reply. "You'll get thousands of pounds for that. Even more in Euros from my native Ireland. "

Stan groaned. "How can I do such a thing? I have to go to school tomorrow and how can I hide that lump of gold as well as try and tell my parents my TV has gone?"

He walked over to the large gold oblong. It was too heavy to lift. He took a blanket from his chest of drawers to cover it. "What happens if my parents see that when I'm at school? They will wonder why I covered my TV."

"Then the miracle will be gone, and the gold will be lost."

"Maybe I don't want any gold."

"Then maybe you don't want me around," Finnian replied sternly, hands on hips.

Stan thought for a bit. Finnian could be very annoying and was making things happen that made his life difficult. Maybe he should tell the leprechaun to take his gold away and never bother him again. He didn't want to lose his friend but also he couldn't upset his parents.

"OK, I'll keep the lump of gold covered, and I'll not tell my parents my TV is missing, so if they see the gold."

"The miracle is undone if they see the gold..." Finnian interrupted. "Plus, you may find yourself befalling terrible luck without me around."

"What kind of bad luck?" Stan was aghast.

"Maybe you don't want to find out," Finnian looked at him seriously. "I suggest you find a way to keep our secret because I warn you, if you lose my miracles, you could lose a lot from your own life". With that he leapt in the air and disappeared in a white flash.

Stan flopped to the floor, holding his head. What could he do about Finnian Coghlan, and how could he handle all this gold?

Stan trudged slowly to school the next day, his hands in his pockets, his head downcast. He wondered about the huge lump of gold in his bedroom that was once his television. It was balanced on the TV stand, and Stan could not lift it an inch. Only his mum went in there to hoover, and if she removed the covering blanket, his secret would be known. If Finnian was telling the truth, the miracle would be undone and bad luck would befall him. Whilst lost in thought, he was suddenly struck from behind by a bicycle on the pavement ridden by another kid going to school. Stan tumbled to the ground and jarred his knee.

"Hey, watch where you're going!" he yelled in annoyance. The lad looked at him, a grim look on his face. He was about to say something nasty, Stan could tell, but then the thug grabbed at his own face as he was unable to open his mouth. The lad, who Stan didn't know other than he was a year above him, was clutching at his mouth with his face reddening, and for a worried moment, Stan was concerned he was having some kind of seizure. Then his eyes drifted across to a nearby lamppost and he saw Finnian Coghlan clinging to it, about halfway up. He was pointing at the boy who'd struck Stan and seemed to be mouthing some kind of spell. Finnian swung his arm to the right, and the boy fell off his bike as if guided by the leprechaun's power. Other children gathered, watching closely and talking excitedly about the peculiar show.

"What happened, Dave?" yelled one of the kids.

Dave got up, shaking his head, and cycled off without a word. Stan sat by the side of the road rubbing his aching knee. He looked back at the lamppost, and Finnian was gone.

Later that evening, Stan sat in silence, eating dinner with his parents. A meal of tofu and vegetables. His parents had raised him a vegetarian and had never given him meat, although unbeknown to them, he'd frequently gone to supermarkets after school to buy pork pies and sausage rolls. He never told them. They wouldn't approve.

Mostly, he was worried about the massive lump of gold in his room. He would surely have to do something about that. He racked his brains for an answer and eventually decided he would have to move it. Then his mum spoke to him.

"Stan, we're going out tonight. Will you be OK on your own this evening? You are ten now so should be able to look after yourself. "

"Yes, perfect," Stan babbled quickly.

"OK, good," his father added.

Later that evening, his parents left, and he dashed to his room to move the lump of gold. He removed the blanket and pulled it to the floor. It landed with a huge crash that knocked a framed picture off the wall. Stan ignored the picture and dragged the gold lump slowly across the floor. It would barely budge, but Stan persisted. He decided he'd take it to the garden shed outside which would require a lot of time and effort, but he had all evening. He managed to push it down the stairs, through the kitchen and out into the garden. For a while, he thought of trying to bury it, but his parents would see the disturbed ground, so he chose not to. His arms aching more than they ever had before he got the gold to the garden shed, dragging it and turning it over. It was now filthy from mud. He realised he couldn't hide it in the shed as his father would find it. He went in there a lot.

Then he looked around the garden and had an idea. Many years ago, Stan had once had a pet dog which had died two years ago, but they'd kept the dog's kennel for sentimental reasons. Stan dragged the gold to the kennel, which his parents never looked at. He doubted they'd get another dog, so he hid it there, lifting the kennel and hiding the gold underneath. His back killed him, but his persistence made sure the gold was hidden. He breathed an exhausted sigh of relief and walked back to the house. Now how would he explain the absent TV? Finnian gave him so many problems!

He returned to his room, replaced the fallen picture, a family photograph taken on holiday, and looked around. He didn't watch TV much but did play computer games on it, and his parents would wonder why it had gone. Maybe he could tell them he'd given up on computer games and put his telly in a skip. A lame excuse, but all he could think of for now. He wondered about the powers of his friend who not only turned things to gold but made a young thug fall off his bike by a movement of his hand. What did Finnian want from a ten-year-old English boy in London? Had he come from Ireland just for him? Too many questions. Stan was tired. He had a shower and went to bed.

Another school week passed without Stan seeing Finnian. Soon, the summer holidays would be when his parents usually took him to Cornwall for a couple of weeks. Right now, it was late May, and the weather was warming considerably. His parents hadn't seen that his TV was missing. His dad rarely went in Stan's room, and his mum had been too busy to hoover and clean in there, so Stan had insisted that he'd do it himself, to which she agreed. He knew he couldn't delay the awkward conversation forever, but for now, he was dealing with it.

That Saturday, he visited his friend Neil, who lived a couple of streets away. Neil came from a poor family and had an older sister who didn't like Stan much. He would usually ignore her as he and Neil played board games and computer games, sometimes with Neil's parents. During a game of chess, Stan strongly considered telling Neil about Finnian Coghlan but remembered the little man's words about bad luck and the reversal of the miracles he'd done for him. Did he really want to keep the gold? He didn't know how to sell it, so it was useless. What did Finnian want from him?

"Checkmate!" Neil yelled happily, startling Stan from his reverie.

"Oh, well done," said Stan, not really too concerned. After a pause, he added. "Neil, what do you think about gold?"

"Gold?" Neil didn't sound interested. "We can't afford gold."

Stan was about to carry on when a movement behind Neil's head shook him. His three-foot, green-suited friend was outside the window, sternly wagging his finger.

"How did you know?" Stan called out in surprise, without really thinking.

"How did I know what?" replied Neil.

"No, I meant... "and then he stopped. Finnian had gone again. Neil looked at where Stan was staring and saw nothing at his window.

"Is something wrong, Stan?" he asked.

"No, forget it," and so he mumbled an excuse and went home. As he walked towards his front door he saw his mother standing outside it. Her face was angry.

"What's the matter, mum?" he asked.

"I think you know," she replied.

Stan cast his eyes downwards. She'd found out about his missing TV, he knew and wondered what excuse he could give.

"Three hundred pounds we paid for your telly, and what have you done with it?"

Stan felt like crying. He didn't know what to say. Then he had a brainwave. "I swapped it," he said.

"Swapped it?"

"Yes, for a. . . for a dartboard," he recalled that he'd had a dartboard as a birthday present from one of his friends. Perhaps his mum had forgotten where he'd got it from.

"Oh, "her face softened a little. "But you could have at least told us. We could have bought you a dartboard, and they don't cost as much as your TV."

Stan sighed. He hated lying, especially to his mum but he was a little uneasy about Finnian and what misfortune the little man could bring him. "I'm sorry," he said.

"Never mind. Come in and have your dinner. Aunt Jenny is here and would like to see you. "

"OK," and he went into the house.

Sunday came and went. A very dull day when the rain didn't stop. He hoped he hadn't upset Finnian. He'd been as honest as he could without causing trouble. He lay in bed looking at the spot where his TV had been, wondering how he could sell his gold without his parents finding out. After all, Finnian said Stan could sell it. He really didn't understand how Finnian wanted him to sell it. Maybe on an internet auction, but he didn't know how they worked. He was only ten. There was no way of talking to anyone about his gold. His family wasn't poor but the gold's value would surely transform their lives.

He fell asleep and went to school the next day. Another rainy day, and he felt very alone. During the lunch break he was talking to a friend by the bike sheds. His friend was smoking even though he was only eleven. Stan hated smoking, as did his parents, but he spoke to his friend Joshua about gold, deciding he didn't care about Mr Coghlan.

"I've got two bars of gold," he blurted out. "Do you know how I could sell them?"

Joshua answered with a mouthful of expletives.

"Seriously" Stan went on. "I've got some gold. "

"How did you get it?" Joshua said.

Stan stopped and thought and realised he had no credible answer. "Oh, never mind," he said and walked away. As he walked past the toilets, he noticed a movement in the doorway. It was the leprechaun.

"I've decided I'll try and help you," the little man said.

Stan stopped and looked at him. "Help with what? You've got me into a lot of trouble, making me lie to my parents."

"I'll help you sell the gold," Finnian said with a wink. "There's a gold dealer a few miles from here, and I will take you there Saturday."

"I can't move the big lump. Only the two small ones," Stan protested.

"Start with them, and we'll do the big one later."

"OK. " Stan felt hugely cheered up. "I'll bring them with me and... " he tailed off as Finnian had gone again. He'd hold him to his word and wait until Saturday.

Saturday morning was bright and sunny. It was now June, and the summer holidays were coming. Stan felt really good as he dressed and wondered where and when little Finnian would show up. After breakfast, Stan told his parents he was going to Neil's house again. They believed him, and he left the house, looking around excitedly for Finnian. It was starting to drizzle, and Stan noticed a rainbow appearing in the sky. He looked at it for a few seconds, and then he felt a hand grab his own hand,

"Quick! We don't have much time!" his friend's voice said, and suddenly, he found himself running through the lanes outside his house. To his amazement, he saw golden lights at the feet of him and Finnian, and then their feet left the ground, and they were headed for the rainbow.

"Have you got the gold?" Finnian said as their ascension grew rapidly.

Stan was too stunned to reply. Of all the miracles he'd seen, this one topped the lot. They were gliding along the top of the rainbow like a waterslide he'd once visited. He had the two gold bars in a backpack, along with some cheese and cucumber sandwiches and a bottle of coke.

"Down we go!" Finnian yelled in delight as they descended into a street in London. It was a deserted street, and as they touched the ground, the rainbow disappeared.

"Wow, that was incredible!" Stan exclaimed. "That's the best thing I've ever done."

Finnian laughed and then pointed to a nearby shop. 'We buy gold,' the shop said, and that was all they needed to know.

"Can I go in on my own?" Stan asked. "It would be strange if they saw you."

"Of course," Finnian replied. "Go ahead."

Stan walked into the shop. He was now holding the two gold bars, one in each hand. A young black man was standing behind the counter, watching him.

"Can I help you?" he said to the boy.

Stan looked through the window at Finnian, who was smiling and putting on a thumbs-up gesture.

"I want to sell some gold," was all he could say, and he handed the man the two bars. The man looked at them and frowned.

"Where did you get these?" he asked.

Stan couldn't think of a reply, so instead, he stammered. "Are. . . er, are they worth anything?"

"If they are not stolen goods, very probably."

"Oh, they're not stolen."

"So where did you get them? A small boy shouldn't be carrying such things. "

"Well I,er... I..." Stan stammered.

The man disappeared from view into a hidden room. Stan bit his fingernails nervously. He could still see Finnian outside the shop. After a few minutes, the man returned and said. "These are each one kilogram of solid gold. They're worth around fifty thousand pounds each."

"Crikey!" Stan gasped.

"Do you seriously think I'll give that kind of money to a kid right now with no background checks? Where are your parents?"

"I can't really explain. . . . er. . . . "

"OK, I'll keep hold of these until I know more," said the man. He turned and disappeared from view. Stan trudged morosely out of the shop to Finnian.

"Well, that was a waste of time," he told the little man.

"Waste of time!" Finnian laughed. "You've just ridden on a rainbow. Not many children get to do that."

"Apart from that."

"Well, what did you expect?"

"Look what is it you want from me?" Stan asked with a sigh.

"I just want you to be my friend. In five thousand years since I was born in Glendalough, I've had just three good friends," Finnian said sadly.

"Oh really?"

"No. O'Reilly was one of them. "

They both looked at each other, and they both laughed.

"Can we ride the rainbow back home?" Stan asked.

"The weather's not right for it," said Finnian.

"So how do we get home? I don't know this area of London. I'm a long way from where I know. "

"You're forgetting, young Stan. I can do miracles. "He reached out for Stan's arm, flickers of light flashed from his hand, and when the light disappeared, they were back in Stan's front garden.

"I'll be off," said Finnian, hopping down the garden path.

Stan couldn't think of a reply, so watched the leprechaun run down the lane and disappear from view. So many thoughts ran through his head, like wondering if he'd see the little man again and how he could deal with that huge lump of gold under the dog kennel. He turned and went back into his house.

The next morning at breakfast, his mother looked at him sternly and said, "You lied to me yesterday. I phoned Neil's parents, and they hadn't seen you all day. Where did you go?"

"Oh, I changed my mind and went to the local football match instead. " Another lie. He was getting used to it now.

"If you keep lying to me, I'll have you grounded," she added and took away the breakfast crockery to the sink.

Stan walked to his room and pondered recent events. He'd got away with the lies about his phone and TV. He'd lost the two lumps of gold to the man in the shop. Finnian was wearying him. So excited by the leprechaun's miracles he couldn't tell him to leave him alone. Life was mostly dull all the time, and Finnian Coghlan was exciting to be around. It was like living in a fun movie. He couldn't believe Finnian was five thousand years old, predating every world religion if that was true. Did he eat and sleep like everyone else? He had the power to teleport himself in flashes of light, to ride rainbows and turn objects into gold as well as knock a spiteful boy off his bike. Stan had never been to Ireland. His parents usually took him to Cornwall, but he did go to Spain when he was five. Travel didn't really interest him. Maybe his friendship with Finnian was over, and he'd never see him again. Lots to ponder, but yet again, school was tomorrow, and he had to prepare for that.

Many months had passed. It was now Christmas, and Stan hadn't seen Finnian. He got a new TV for Christmas but wasn't excited by it. Sometimes, he cried, particularly on rainy days. Every now and then, he'd look under the dog kennel to see if the gold was still there. Always it was, but he had no idea what to do with it. On the new year's eve, he decided he couldn't hold on any longer and he said to his parents. "There is something in the dog kennel I want to show you. " His father looked at him and raised an eyebrow. "Like what?" he said... Stan led his parents to the garden and lifted the kennel, but the gold was gone. His old TV was there instead.

"That's your TV!" his mother gasped. "So you've been lying again."

Stan was too depressed to care. The miracle was undone. Finnian was gone, possibly forever. He passively listened to his parents scolding him for a few minutes without really listening or replying. It was all over.

Fifteen years later, Stan got married, and when his first son was born, he called him Finnian. He'd never forget his childhood friend and their adventures, but it was time to be a responsible grown-up and move on. Thinking of Finnian got him through many lonely times in his youth, but he liked being a husband and father and was happy to leave behind the things of his childhood. One day in his thirties he visited Glendalough in Ireland, where Finnian said he was born but never saw him again. Standing by Glendalough Lake, he saw a small green top hat floating in the water, and he wondered if his miraculous friend would last forever. The wonders of childhood, but it was time to move on.

24.

Enrique Sanchez and Miguel Fernandez carefully manoeuvred the heavy box from the back of the car and walked slowly up the hill with it in that remote part of the Scottish Highlands. It was a sunny spring day, and both men from Colombia were pleased with finding the cave to conceal their massive haul of cocaine. They had searched for the right cave for many hours. Over forty kilograms in the wooden box, and Miguel, a slim man aged forty slipped a few times as they brought it to the cave entrance. They settled it on the ground for a brief rest.

"Plenty of hard work, Enrique," said Miguel, wiping his brow.

"All worth it, Miguel," replied his companion. "We make a big fortune. A big fortune in Scotland."

Enrique was also aged forty. He had a thick black moustache, unlike his clean-shaven associate. After a thirty-second breather, they picked up the box again and moved it further into the cave.

"Bit of a bad smell in here," Miguel said. "Like rotten meat."

"Don't worry about the smell. Think of the smell of the money," Enrique answered, grinning. "We can make millions in the Scottish cities."

Both men sat down on rocks by the cave's entrance and began smoking. They looked at their nearby car parked some twenty metres away. Nobody could disturb them here.

The cave seemed to extend deep into the mountain, where the two drug runners did not want to take their box and become lost. They watched an eagle circling overhead. A slight breeze ruffled their clothes as they puffed serenely on their cigarettes.

Both men seemed oblivious to a thudding noise from deep within the cave, like heavy footsteps. Then, other noises, like growling and groaning, became apparent. Both men expected it to be the sounds of some wild Scottish animal. They paid no heed to it, but then came a voice.

"What are you doing in my cave?" it roared.

Miguel and Enrique looked at each other for a second and then into the dark recess of the cave. "Who's there?" shouted Miguel, getting to his feet. He flung his cigarette butt away.

"Get out of my cave!" the voice snarled again, and then both men saw the source of this voice. Enrique also leapt to his feet,

A large man, or what at first seemed like a man, loomed out of the darkness. He was impossibly tall. Over seven feet in height, completely bald with light brown skin and only wearing a loincloth made of what looked like the hide from a deer. In one hand, he held a huge spiked club and in the other, the severed leg of a sheep that dripped blood on the floor.

"Caramba! What is that?" Miguel exclaimed.

"Get out!" the large visitor shouted, and he swung his club, which struck the box on the floor—clouds of white cocaine puffed in the air for a second.

"Let's get out of here!" Enrique cried, and both men ran to their car. They didn't look back until they reached it, but the person or creature did not follow them. They looked at the cave and each other.

"What do we do?" Miguel asked, shaking a little.

"I don't know. It looked like a yeti or something that didn't exist." They heard no further sounds other than that of the soft breeze.

"I'll take him down with my 9mm," Miguel said. "He might steal our stash. "

The Colombian reached into the front of the car and pulled out the gun. Both men cautiously walked towards the cave, expecting to be confronted again. They reached the cave entrance and saw their container of drugs with a big dent in its side. Some of the powder was trickling onto the floor. They saw nobody, but as they listened, they could hear some sort of conversation going on. It came from further into the cave's darkness, and they could make out a shrill voice in an Irish accent. Then they heard a reply, the booming voice of the person or thing that had threatened them earlier. They could not make out the words and so stepped further in.

"Got you!" a voice yelled in triumph, and from the side of the cave, a wooden club descended onto Miguel's hand holding the gun. He screamed and dropped it, and then, holding his injured arm, he ran towards the cave entrance. Swiftly, Enrique grabbed the fallen weapon, raised it and fired into the darkness. Silence for a few seconds. Then, a sound like laughter. Enrique stepped backwards, keeping his gun pointed into the gloom ahead. Somebody emerged from the cave's blackness, a very tiny man in a green suit wearing a green top hat. He was shaking his head and waving his finger.

"Now, you'll not be using such nasty weapons against my friend Egor. This is his cave, and you don't belong here. "he said.

Dumbfounded, Enrique didn't reply and kept the gun pointed at the stranger. The little man, three feet in height, walked over to the damaged box the men had brought in and pulled off its lid, exposing the numerous clear plastic bags. "And you'll not be distributing this filth to the good people of Scotland," he went on.

That was too much for Enrique, and he fired the gun at the little man. With lightning speed, the visitor held out his left hand and both watching men gasped as they saw the bullet drop to the floor, the gunshot resounding noisily around the cave.

"No way!" Enrique yelled. Then, more movement as behind the little man appeared the seven-foot beast in front of them.

"What's happening, Finnian?" he gurgled.

"These vile men were just leaving, weren't you, fellas?" Finnian replied, and without another word the two Colombians fled in terror out of the cave. Finnian and Egor watched them sprinting madly towards their parked car. They got in but didn't drive off and instead sat there motionless, staring out of the windows in shock.

"Such dreadful people, Egor," the little man said and Egor grinned a large toothless grin, saliva dripping from his mouth. He took a large bite from the sheep's leg and then held out the leg to Finnian.

Finnian shook his head. "No thanks. I'm trying to go vegetarian. " Egor snorted in disgust and took another bite.

"We've got to do something about this awful pile of powder they've brought in. " Finnian said, shaking his head. After a pause, he clicked his fingers and smiled in delight. "I know just what to do. "He then ventured to the back of the cave and brought out a full-length mirror that had been left there some years ago. "We'll take this awful stuff and pass it into the spirit world where those lowlifes can't get to it. "

Egor didn't really understand, and so just grunted in agreement. He walked towards the front of the cave, where there was now a faint drizzle and then recoiled as another gunshot rang out.

"Urgh!" he groaned and stepped back.

"What awful beasts those men are, Egor. They give ogres like you a bad name. " Finnian squealed. He then removed his hat and scratched his bald head thoughtfully. "Egor, do me a favour and rip the side of this box off, can you please?"

Egor grabbed the wooden box and wrenched it off the side of it, which noisily splintered into fragments in front of them. The plastic bags within began to slide out onto the cave floor. Finnian picked several of them up and took them to the mirror. He then smiled as they disappeared into its reflective surface like a shimmering pool of water. He made several journeys while Egor watched in silent contemplation as he munched on the leg of the sheep he'd stolen from the hillside. One by one, the bags of powder slid away, and eventually, Finnian was left with the last two bags and as he walked towards the mirror the two men appeared at the front of the cave.

"Give us back our drugs, or we will kill you!" snarled Miguel

Finnian and Egor glanced at each other. Enrique pointed the gun again.

"There's two bags left, fellas. The rest are in the mirror," Finnian replied, laughing. "What do you mean, you crazy little man?" Enrique answered.

"You can't shoot me. I'm indestructible like all leprechauns are."

"I can shoot him, though," growled Enrique, and he fired the gun at Egor. The ogre howled in pain as the bullet struck his shoulder, and he fell to the ground, dropping his club and the sheep's leg. Finnian pushed the last two bags of cocaine into the mirror, and then he leapt at Enrique, knocking him to the ground.

"I'll be taking this now, you cowardly beast," he yelled at the Colombian and grabbing the gun from him, he ran to the mirror and, as with the drugs, made it disappear out of sight.

Miguel and Enrique ran towards him. Their fear was overcome.

Black blood oozed from Egor's wound, but the ogre reached out with his club from the floor and caused the two men to stumble over it, after which he got up and grabbed them around the shoulders. He then held them, spluttering and cursing in the air in front of Finnian.

He stood before them, his face stern. "Now, you boys need to be taught a lesson," he said, waving his finger accusingly. "If you really want that filth, you can go into the spirit world with it. "He pointed at the mirror.

Neither of the men answered. Both were suspended in the air in front of the annoyed leprechaun and writhed in discomfort.

"Or," he went on. "You can both go back to your car, drive away and never involve yourselves in such business again. " Some of Egor's blood was running into their clothes, but neither of them noticed. After a while, Finnian made a gesture to Egor, and the creature dropped the two drug dealers to the ground. They sank to their knees, breathing heavily.

"OK, Egor, do the honours," said Finnian, stepping away from the mirror.

The ogre grunted, picked up his fallen club, and swung it at the mirror, smashing it to pieces.

Seeing this, the two men got to their feet and ran out of the cave. They'd lost their drugs and their gun but didn't want to lose their lives. Finnian and Egor walked to the cave entrance and watched as the two criminals hastily clambered into their car and drove away.

"Are you badly hurt, Egor?" Finnian asked the towering figure. "A little magic fairy dust should do the trick. "He then reached into his pocket and flung a handful of gold-coloured dust over his friend. The gunshot wound began to disappear, and Egor grinned in delight.

"Thanks, buddy," Egor responded. Picking up the fallen leg of the sheep, he lumbered away into the dark recesses of the cave.

25.

It was 3 am in the morning in late July when two men were walking across the grass in Phoenix Park Dublin, each holding a bottle of their favourite moonshine in their hands. These were no ordinary men. They were leprechauns who were thousands of years old. They sat down on the grass near the huge white papal cross erected in 1979 and began a discussion.

"You know what, Brian?" Finnian said—the eldest of the two at five thousand years old.

"What's that Finnian?" Brian replied, swigging from his bottle. He was a youngster at three thousand years old. Unlike Finnian, he had no facial hair, but also wore entirely green clothes.

"I think if I could deal with the boredom, I'd be happy to be here forever."

Brian laughed. "I know what you mean. When you think about how short human life is, they're always wailing about how bored they are. "

"I mean, what is the purpose of a universe that isn't eternal, Brian? Shakespeare spoke about the dream after death. That's something I can admire about an English man, although there's not a lot else."

"Yes, it's all a dream, Finnian. Dreams can kill boredom the way Poitin does for me. I suspect you must forget much of what you've lived through to enjoy going on forever."

"I remember an awful lot, a young man from five thousand years of experience. A lot of it belongs in the past and should stay forgotten, but sometimes the memories bubble up. "

"Everyone you ever love will pass away while you carry on with whoever else that's capable of going with you if anyone does. "

"Good grief, Brian, it's a bleak prospect. "

"I suppose intelligence is a curse as well as a blessing, Finnian. "

They both watched as a plane passed overhead. All lit up and making a faint noise.

"The advancement of human endeavour to the sacrificing of all that was beautiful about an unsullied natural world is quite sad," said Finnian, taking a swig of poitin.

"The 20th century was devastating, my friend. The most enlightened and destructive time in the history of all creation. They put up a cross here for Jesus and the Pope. Jesus only helps people when they're dead; by then, it's too late."

"So what are you saying, Brian? God won't help us when we're alive?"

"A lot of people get no help when they're alive. Not from God anyway, and how many painful and lonely deaths have happened since the painful death of poor Jesus?"

"Too many to mention my friend. "

Brian stood up and yawned. "It's great that we've got each other, my good friend," he said. "Going on forever, rather like death, is only bearable if you are not alone. "

"We're not going to die Brian," said Finnian, also standing up. "We're the enchanted ones, like eternal childhood, and nothing can get rid of us. "

The two little men walked towards the white cross.

"It's a beautiful thing," Finnian said, looking up at the cross. Stars blazed over the sky above it. "What's beautiful? The cross?"

"The world beneath the stars is the most beautiful thing of all. I fear for our future, Brian. It doesn't take much to render a life form extinct. The dinosaurs were bold and beautiful like humans, but all had to go."

"The dinosaurs never had our sophisticated brains, so they couldn't contemplate their demise as we can," Brian said sadly, stumbling slightly at the effects of his drink.

"Humans can feel love, as can us sophisticated leprechauns. Love is what created the industrial revolution. A desire to selflessly help and serve our fellow humans. Yet the damage to the environment is immeasurable, and what love can repair it?"

"You've got me there, Finnian Coghlan."

"I really love Dublin, but I've met a lot of children in England. Sometimes, I think that's the best place in the world to be a child. Do you agree, Brian?"

"Aye, or the UK in general. There's a real appreciation of childhood there, to be sure. "

"The love for children in England is like the industrial revolution. A huge, powerful juggernaut of activity unlike anything else. "

Brian took a big gulp of his moonshine and belched loudly. "But what can we do, Finnian? So much to do and so little time to do it."

"Brian O'Reilly, you're the eternal pessimist. As there will always be children, there will always be the seeds of a revolution. Children don't feel the anxieties of the adult. They never look back with regret. It's always about the future of children. That's how the human race needs to develop. That's why people like you and me exist."

"So we're not the figment of somebody's wild imagination, Finnian? We're really here."

"And we're here forever my friend," Finnian added, reaching out his bottle to clink with Brian's. "The universe threw us into existence, and we've too much love to give for it to ever disappear."

"I'll drink to that old buddy," Brian said with a laugh and the two ancient friends carried on walking along in Phoenix park next to the huge white cross.

26.

It was at around 2 am that the pub owner, Dean Block, heard the tapping noise. The pub had been empty since the last reveller had left two hours ago. He'd been cleaning glasses and putting things away tidily for the preparation for the next day. It was a Friday night, and would be busy again Saturday. At first, he thought the noise could be rats in the cellar, but they'd never been there before in the ten years he'd owned the pub he ran with his wife.

Tap, tap, tap. Then, a pause. Then tap tap tap again. He caught a glimpse of himself in the mirror behind the bar. Bald and overweight, with bulging veins on his forehead. He looked every inch the 59-year-old he was. He wasn't used to stress, but that noise was getting him stressed. He was a heavy drinker himself but had never had hallucinations, which he associated with drugs he had never tried.

Eventually, he flung the cleaning cloth on the bar and sighed heavily. He would have to find out what that sound was, or it would drive him crazy. It was coming from the cellar, so he opened the cellar door and peered in. The tapping sound grew louder and seemed to be accompanied by singing. Surely not! Who had got into his cellar unseen?

"Hello! Who's there?" he called.

The tapping stopped. So did the singing. "Hello!" he repeated. Silence.

"OK, I'm coming in," he called, cautiously descending the stone staircase.

He flicked on the light switch and looked around. At first, everything seemed how it should be, the beer barrels against the wall. Nothing out of place.

"Bah!" he cried, and he turned to leave, but then a movement in the furthest corner of the cellar caught his eye. "What's that?" he called. "Who's there?"

"Don't hit me!" a voice called back. A voice he'd never heard before.

Dean stared ahead and he could make out someone in the corner, an absurdly tiny man in a green suit holding a tiny hammer kneeling in front of two pairs of bright green shoes.

"Who are you?" he shouted. "What are you doing in my pub's cellar?"

The man stood up, and Dean gasped. The stranger was barely three feet tall, had a thick ginger-coloured beard, and was unlike anyone he'd seen before. His piercing green eyes stared at him with serene wisdom. "Forgive me, sir," the little man answered, his voice strongly Irish in accent. "I was making two pairs of shoes as it's something I used to do before I got rich and yet will still. . . "

"I don't care about that," the man interrupted sternly. "Please get out of my pub, or I will throw you out myself. " "Goodness me, how rude!" the visitor exclaimed. "Don't you wish to buy a pair of shoes? The ones with yellow laces can make you levitate, while the ones with blue laces can make you invisible. I've just finished the work on them. " "What rubbish are you talking about?" the landlord spat contemptuously. "Do you want me to call the police?"

"Call the police on poor old Finnian?" he replied sadly. "What?"

"That's my name. Finnian Coghlan and I thought…"

"Look, get out!" the pub owner yelled. "It's too late, and I'm too tired."

"I think you need to learn some manners," Finnian said calmly, his hands on his hips. "Watch this!"

Dean stared in annoyance and then felt what seemed like a powerful gust of wind that knocked him to the floor. As he lay on his back, stricken and aching, the peculiar stranger ran over to him, grabbing the shoes with yellow laces from the ground. Before he had time to react, Dean saw his old shoes pulled off and the yellow-laced green ones placed there instead. They fit perfectly.

"What have you done?" He cried out and got awkwardly to his feet, which wasn't easy as he was a big man. He looked down at the odd-looking shoes, and then a few seconds later, something incredible happened, and he felt himself lifting upwards from the floor. He ascended at least two feet from the ground.

"Aaaah!" he screamed.

"As you can see, these shoes can make you levitate," the stranger said matter-of-factly. "Normally, I would charge a million Euros for them. Sorry, not Euros but pounds as we're in England now. "

Dean floated up to the stone ceiling, and he put his hands up to prevent his head from banging against it.

"As you're not being a friendly man I will not let you have them for free, but I thought you should try before you buy."

"This is madness!" he shouted from the ceiling. "I must be dreaming."

"We use Euros in Ireland now. I expect you to know that. I doubt you can afford the asking price running a cheap place like this. "

Finnian watched the stricken man, his arms folded. "The shoes with the blue laces can make you invisible. Us leprechauns are masters of invisibility when it suits us. That's why so few people see us and, therefore, don't believe in us. "

"Please!" Dean gasped. "Let me down."

"OK," Finnian went on. "The invisibility shoes cost two million pounds. Oh, I don't need the money, don't get me wrong. It's just a hobby I have. "

At that moment, the man in the air spun upside down, his shoes pointing at the ceiling.

"OK, I think you've suffered enough," Finnian said, and he grabbed the man's dangling hands and pulled him down to the floor. His peculiar shoes popped off as he did so and landed neatly on the floor next to each other. Dean lay face down on the ground, wheezing heavily.

"What the hell just happened?" he groaned.

"You've witnessed the power of the leprechauns," came the reply.

"There's no such thing," he said, dragging himself to his feet. "I must have had my drink spiked or something. None of this is possible."

"Everything is possible with the little people," Finnian said with a laugh.

Dean stared at the visitor, still wheezing. "Was I wearing magic shoes?" he asked, rubbing sweat from his brow.

"Absolutely," Finnian said proudly. "I made them myself. Only me and my good friend Brian O'Reilly know how to make them as all the others have forgotten the secret."

"The shoes made me float in the air! That felt incredible."

"Would you like to try on the invisibility shoes and surprise your friends?" Finnian asked. He picked up the pair of shoes from the floor and held them up to him.

Dean shook his head and took a few steps back. "You've scared me enough already. I just want a normal life." "Normal. Also known as boring. Suit yourself."

"You want millions of pounds for them. I can't afford that anyway."

Finnian laughed and then looked around the cellar. His eyes lit up at the sight of something in the corner. "Well, look at this!" he exclaimed, running over to it.

"Look at what?" replied Dean.

"A big box of bottles of poteen!The leprechauns' favourite drink!"

"Yes we've been stocking it lately, but don't get much demand for it."

The leprechaun looked at him, grinning. "I'll tell you what," he said. "I'll trade you both pairs of magic shoes for this box of poteen."

"The magic shoes? Ones you said could make you invisible?"

"Indeed, I did say that! So you can go out and help yourself with all the money you'll ever need. Plus, with the other shoes, you can float in the air."

"I thought you wanted millions of pounds."

"I'm in a generous mood, Mr Block, so what do you say?"

The landlord rubbed his head, looking at the shoes on the floor and the strange little man. "OK, it's a deal," he said.

"Splendid!" cried the leprechaun, and he lifted the box of about ten bottles off the floor. "I'll be seeing you then. I'll let myself out. "

He then slowly ascended the stairs carrying the awkward plywood box.

Dean watched him go, and as he disappeared from sight, he called out. "How did you even get in here in the first place?"

There was no answer and he looked back at the shoes on the floor. They were both bright green in colour but looked just like ordinary lace-up shoes. They appeared to be made of some kind of thick leather, but it was hard to tell. He picked them up and saw no distinguishing marks on them. He thought about trying them on but instead thought he'd surprise his wife in the morning with them. He left the cellar with the shoes and, after locking up the pub, walked across the street to his house opposite. When he got home, his wife was already asleep in bed, so he placed the shoes on the floor next to the bed and decided to wait until the morning.

The following morning, after breakfast, Dean stared at his wife, Pamela, with a big grin on his face. Eventually, she sighed and exclaimed. "Look, what is it?"

"I've got a surprise for you, Pam," he said. "I've found a way for us both to get fabulously rich. " "Really? How?"

"Wait here a minute," he said and went upstairs to bring down the leprechaun's shoes. He showed them to her while she stared at him with puzzlement.

"These are magic shoes!" he said happily. "One pair can make me levitate, and the other pair can make me invisible. " "What nonsense, Dean!" she replied. "What were you drinking last night?"

"I'll show you," he said, taking off his slippers and putting on the shoes with the yellow laces that had caused him to levitate. As before, they fitted perfectly. After putting them on, he stood up and grinned, holding his arms aloft. Nothing happened, and Dean's grin faded.

"What's going on?" he yelled in annoyance and jumped in the air—still nothing.

"Why the double-crossing…" he shouted and took the shoes off. He put the other pair of shoes on, which also fitted perfectly, and he stared at his wife. "Can you see me?" he asked.

"Of course I can, you gormless oaf," she replied. "Why shouldn't I?"

"That little weirdo tricked me!" he said, pulling off the shoes and hurling them to the floor. "Now I've lost a nice stock of finest poteen for nothing."

He sat down at the kitchen table and put his head in his hands. After several seconds of silence, their phone rang in the corner. His wife walked over to it and picked it up.

"Hello," she answered.

Dean got up and snatched the phone from her. "Hello," he repeated, and then he stopped. From the phone's earpiece, they both heard high-pitched mocking laughter.